For Eva and Arthur

Acknowledgements

Thank you to all my family and friends who have offered encouragement and support during the writing of this book.

Special thanks to the pupils and teachers of Primary Six at Portree Primary School for their enthusiasm about the early drafts of this book and for all their helpful comments along the way.

And I'd also like to thank my wonderful editor and alchemist of prose, John Hudspith, a stern but constructive critic who accepts nothing but the best, and book designer, Jane Dixon-Smith, who has ensured the book looks good both inside and out.

Chapter One

Caitlin Cameron had just woken up and even before she opened her eyes, she realised she was bored. She decided to try reading a book. Granny Skye always advised reading a book when bored. But the book, which had been a present from her granny, and was called *Heroines and Heroes of History*, didn't hold her attention and she soon let it slip onto the floor.

It was the fifth week of the summer holidays. Caitlin liked the holidays and didn't want them to be over, especially as when they *were* over she'd be starting at Burgh High. She was going to miss Southside Primary and Miss Stewart. But liking the holidays didn't stop her being bored at times. So, today, what could she do today?

Rain pattered against her bedroom window. The weather on Skye had been lovely. Caitlin and her father had been for their holidays. They'd stayed with Granny and Granddad Chisholm, or Granny Skye and Seanair, as Caitlin called her grandparents. They'd only just got back to Edinburgh a couple of days ago and it had been raining since they crossed the Forth Bridge.

She picked up the little black velvet box from her bedside table. She opened the box and looked at the silver locket that lay on the white, silk lining. Granny Skye had given it to her a few days earlier.

"I think now's the time to pass it on," Granny had said. She'd handed over the heart-shaped locket like it was something breakable. "Look after it, Caitlin, it's very precious. It's so precious that some people think it should be in a museum."

"In a museum? Why?"

"Because it's nearly three hundred years old and it belonged to our ancestor Flora Macdonald. She was given it by Bonnie Prince Charlie in 1746. It's been handed down through the family ever since and it's been worn at all sorts of special occasions. Your mum wore it when she married your dad. She gave it back to me when she knew— well— you know..."

Caitlin looked at her granny's sad face and the big lump of sadness in her tummy moved. *Oh, no you don't,* she said to the lump. *You stay where you are.* She pressed her lips together and looked up at the ceiling.

Granny grabbed her in a big hug. "Sorry, my darling. I didn't mean to upset you, mentioning your mum. But I think she'd like you to have it now. So, will you take it, look after it?"

Caitlin wondered why Granny didn't give it to Auntie Morag or Auntie Flossie, they were Mum's big sisters after all. But she didn't ask. "Okay," she said "But who's Bonnie Prince Charlie?"

Granny raised her eyebrows. "What on earth do they teach you at that school of yours? You don't know about Bonnie Prince Charlie?"

"I think I've heard of him, but I don't know anything about him."

Granny gave Caitlin a funny look. "Right, my girl! I know where we're taking you today. I'll just tell Seanair to hurry up with the sheep and then we'll be on our way."

And a little while later, Caitlin and her grandparents were on the road to Inverness to visit Culloden, the place where Prince Charlie had fought and lost his last battle in his struggle to become the king of the United Kingdom.

Caitlin hadn't been sure what to expect, but the Culloden Centre turned out to be a really cool place and Granny had made the story of the Bonnie Prince sound exciting and interesting. The Prince hadn't succeeded in replacing King George but he had been a real big hero to lots of people. Caitlin ended up feeling proud that she was related to Flora Macdonald. Flora had helped the Prince to escape after the battle, maybe even saved his life. Not only that, but now Caitlin had something which had once belonged to both Flora and the Prince. And that was pretty cool.

And now, sitting in her bed, Caitlin ran her finger over the locket's heart-shaped surface. She traced the tiny flower pattern that was engraved on it. Then, very carefully, she opened it up and looked again at the small painted picture behind the glass. It was a picture of Prince Charlie's face. He really did look quite handsome. Caitlin could see why he'd been called 'bonnie'.

Granny had given her strict instructions that she wasn't to wear the locket, except on very special occasions, and that she should wait until she was a bit older before wearing it outside.

However, now she was back home, Caitlin really wanted to show it to her friends. Then she had an idea. She would take a photo of it. She'd got a new phone from her dad for her birthday just a few weeks before and it took really good pictures.

After she'd taken a couple of shots of the locket, she decided to give her book another try. She picked it up off the floor and opened it. She yawned as she lay back on her pillow and began reading.

As she read, she could hear her dad getting ready for work, heard him singing in the shower, in the room below hers, and then whistling as he got dressed. Caitlin wasn't sure when it was that Dad had started singing and whistling again. It gave her a mixed-up feeling to hear him, sort of happy and cross at the same time. She hoped it didn't mean he was forgetting about Mum. She knew *she* would never forget. She knew *she* would always miss Mum. She also knew she'd always be angry her mum had died. Too late, Caitlin felt hot tears on her face. She rubbed at them with her fists. She would not cry, no matter what all the grown-ups said about it being okay. It was not okay, Caitlin knew that if she started, she wouldn't be able to stop.

After looking at the ceiling and concentrating on her breathing for a few minutes, the need to cry was gone. She got out of bed, opened the curtains and was glad to see it had stopped raining. At least she could get out of the house.

"Caitlin, can you come down please!" Dad's voice bellowed up two flights of stairs.

As she pulled on jeans and her favourite blue hoodie, she heard the doorbell ring. *Probably the postman,* she thought, as she clattered down the stairs

But it wasn't the postman who'd been at the door. They had a visitor, a visitor who was sitting at their kitchen table.

Oh no, NO, Caitlin thought. *Not her. Dad hadn't, had he? No, he couldn't have.*

But he had.

"Ah, Caitlin," Dad said, smiling. "Come and meet Miss Blawearie, your new childminder."

Caitlin stared at her father, eyes wide in alarm. Dad put his arm around her shoulders. "Don't look so worried," he said. "I know you're going to miss Susie. But you knew the agency would be sending someone today, to fill the gap until they can get a permanent replacement."

Caitlin nodded. "I hate when people go away," she whispered. "I miss you when you're at work and now Susie's gone and, and..."

Dad stroked her cheek. "I know. I'm sorry, sweetheart. I wish it didn't have to be this way." Dad looked as sad as Caitlin felt.

She didn't mean to make him sad. She loved her dad very

much. He was a great dad—kind, a bit strict sometimes, but a bit daft and funny too.

But what was he thinking of? This couldn't be her childminder. This person, who was standing there watching Caitlin and her dad, who was wearing her usual long, purple velvet coat and purple, Peruvian-style hat—was Scary Lady. That's what all the kids called her. And who wears a long coat and a hat with earflaps in July anyway? Never mind all the other weird things about her.

"Bella Blawearie," Scary Lady said, placing her large black velvet shoulder bag on the table and offering an outstretched hand to Caitlin.

Caitlin glanced at the bag. There was a picture of a clock face sewn into the black material. The hands were at five-to-twelve. She looked at Scary Lady. "Hello," she said, forcing herself to offer her hand.

Scary Lady grabbed hold of it and shook it up and down. "Pleased to meet you," she said. Caitlin noticed that actually her eyes were merry and kind-looking. And although the woman's long fingers were thin and cold, Caitlin was surprised that her nails were varnished red and on her index finger was a ring. A ring set with a big, orangey-brown stone.

Caitlin tried to return the smile, but didn't quite manage it. The woman released her hand and stepped away, looking Caitlin up and down. Caitlin stared back.

"And this," Miss Blawearie said, stepping to one side, and waggling a hand behind her, "is Jack—Jack Russell." A small, black, brown and white dog scuttled out from under the chair Scary Lady had been sitting on. His stiff little tail wagged and he sat there, looking up at Caitlin with one of his front paws raised. "He's pleased to meet you. Why don't you shake his paw."

Caitlin's father didn't really like dogs and wouldn't let Caitlin have one no matter how much she pleaded. He was a doctor, which meant he cared far too much about germs.

Surely he wasn't going to let this woman bring her dog to the house every day. She glanced at her father. He looked a bit uncomfortable but he just smiled and nodded. Caitlin supposed he was being polite and didn't want to upset Scary Lady and have her leave—although Caitlin wouldn't have minded. But the dog really was very sweet. She bent down and took the dog's paw in her hand. His tail continued to wag.

"Jack—Caitlin. Caitlin—Jack," Scary Lady made the introductions.

Caitlin straightened up. "So he's a—"

"Jack Russell—yes. I know the name may not seem very imaginative, but it just seemed simpler. I like to keep things simple whenever possible."

"Right," Caitlin said, thinking it was just as well not everyone did the same. Or it could get confusing. She wondered if Scary Lady would call a Labrador, Labrador and a Collie, Collie.

"Miss Blawearie." Dad was holding up the teapot. "Would you like a cup?"

"Oh, yes please. And Jack should have some water." She reached into her bag and produced a small plastic bowl. She held it out to Caitlin. "Would you mind?"

"Oh, right," said Caitlin, still feeling a bit dazed. She took the bowl and went to the sink to fill it. As she laid the bowl on the floor, Scary Lady reached into her bag again. This time she took out a cup and saucer—white china decorated with little pink roses—and placed them on the table.

Dad looked a little surprised but began pouring.

"I can't stand mugs—thick horrible things," Scary Lady said. "And I'm glad to see you use a pot, just a pity it's teabags and not the real thing. But I'll make the best of it."

Dad gave a small nod and a smile. "You sound like my mother-in-law," he said. "Help yourself to milk." He pushed the carton towards her.

She sniffed and raised her eyebrows.

"Sorry," said Dad. "You'd probably prefer it in a jug. I'm sure we have one somewhere."

Miss Blawearie raised a hand. "No, don't trouble yourself. I know you need to get off to work and like I said, I make the best of things. Sugar would be nice though." She looked around, her hand still in the air. Then she rummaged in her bag again. This time she produced one of those snowstorm ornament things, the kind you shake and artificial snow falls on a wintry scene. Bella shook it. Caitlin tried to see what was inside the glass but the snow seemed to keep swirling. All she could see was what appeared to be a flash of tartan.

Scary Lady peered at the dome and then glanced down at her bag. "Hmm," she said. "It's later than I thought."

Dad glanced at the kitchen clock. "Yes, I better get going—first day back—shouldn't be late. Surgery will be busy. Caitlin, could you find some sugar? And there's cereal for you on the table." He kissed the top of her head. " I love you. See you later. Be good." Then he wrapped Caitlin in one of his huge bear hugs.

She hugged him back and for a few precious moments she enjoyed his lovely daddy-smell. "Love you too, Dad," she said.

He let her go and smiled his lovely, sort of sad, daddy smile. "Caitlin will keep you right, Miss Blawearie. I'll be back around five, and you have my number." And then he was gone.

"So, sugar?" said Scary Lady.

Caitlin dug around in the kitchen cupboards until she found a bag of sugar. She plonked it down on the table.

"Why thank you, but no bowl?" Miss Blawearie smiled.

And again Caitlin noticed she had friendly, twinkly eyes. "Bowl? Eh, no," Caitlin said.

"Not to worry, I'll make the best of it." Scary Lady reached into her bag once more.

Oh no, she couldn't have, could she? But no, no sugar bowl emerged. However, she did produce a silver teaspoon, and put three heaped spoons of sugar into her cup.

Caitlin, meanwhile, looked at the cereal Dad had put out for her. Cornflakes. She didn't like cornflakes. That was what her big brother James ate. She'd told Dad, told him her favourite was Cheerios. But unless she went with him to the supermarket he never remembered. Mum had never forgotten. The lump of sadness moved again in Caitlin's stomach.

"Hot buttered toast, I think, don't you?" Scary Lady clapped her hands twice and stood up. "A fresh pot of tea too. Your father's brew is rather weak. Tea you can stand a spoon in, that's what's needed."

Caitlin found herself staring again. Scary Lady was very tall, and on her feet—yes, they really were biker boots she was wearing.

"And you may call me Bella. Scary Lady seems a bit rude after all."

"What? How did you—?"

"Oh, there's not much that I don't know. And I'll bet you don't like being called Ginger Cat, do you?"

Caitlin gasped and her hand went to her hair. She hated her nickname. She couldn't help her hair colour and, besides, she liked it. Mum had had red hair too.

"So, you call me Bella and I'll call you Caitlin." Bella's eyes beamed and twinkled. "And you're right to be proud of your hair."

Caitlin couldn't speak. This woman seemed to be able to see inside her head.

While she waited for the kettle to boil, Bella took off her coat and hat and put them on one of the kitchen chairs.

Caitlin could only gawp—again. Bella's hair was red, not ginger red like Caitlin's, but scarlet red and it was very short and spiky. Caitlin had expected it to be grey. And in her ears, Bella wore big golden hoops. But the surprise of the hair and earrings were nothing compared to the shock of what Bella was wearing. Bella's top was a black tee-shirt with a picture of Edinburgh castle on it and this was teamed with a short kilt and tartan tights. And then there were the biker boots. Without the coat she looked even taller and thinner than before. Caitlin thought Bella must be at least as tall as Dad. But, even more surprising than all that, was that without the coat and hat, Bella looked a lot younger. She was only 'Dad old' and not as Caitlin had at first thought, 'Granny old'.

Soon Bella and Caitlin were sitting facing each other at the kitchen table and munching gorgeously, butter-meltingly, warm toast.

"You have very pretty eyes," Bella said, between mouthfuls of toast and sips of tea. "The perfect match for your hair—amber like my ring." Bella pointed to the ring Caitlin had noticed earlier. "Striking isn't it?"

"It's— it's very—big," Caitlin said, thinking it was actually quite ugly.

"Oh, it's not to everyone's taste, I know, but this ring goes back a long way. It belonged to my mother, my grandmother, great-grandmother, all the way back through my family to the eighteenth century. This ring has history. Do you know history, Caitlin? Do you know how important it is?" Bella popped a last morsel of toast into her mouth and downed the rest of her tea —all the time gazing intently at Caitlin.

Then Caitlin remembered. "Bonnie Prince Charlie!" she said. "He was in history—Scottish history—and English too, I suppose. Granny told me about him. Her and Seanair, they took me to the Culloden Centre in Inverness to see stuff about his life."

Bella's eyebrows shot up. "Really! They did? Well, that's excellent news."

"And Granny gave me a silver locket. She said it belonged to the Prince and that he gave it to my ancestor Flora Macdonald."

"She did! Even better!" Bella clasped her hands together and smiled her twinkly smile. "I love it when my plans come together."

Chapter Two

"Here comes Edward now," Lynette said, pirouetting around the swing that Caitlin was sitting on. Lynette went to ballet and highland dancing lessons and she was always practising.

After breakfast, the rain had stopped and the sun had come out. Caitlin asked if she could go out to play. Bella said she thought that was a very good idea. She said to Caitlin to take her mobile phone, and to come home for lunch at one o'clock.

Caitlin had immediately texted her two best friends, Lynette and Edward, and asked them to meet her at the swing park. She hadn't seen them for two whole weeks and she'd missed them, although she wasn't sure how to tell them about her new childminder.

Just before Lynette announced Edward's arrival, Caitlin had been watching Lynette as she danced and pranced and she'd been thinking how pretty her friend looked. But then, Lynette always looked pretty. Her blonde hair was always perfectly straightened, unlike Caitlin's mass of tight ginger curls. And Lynette always wore lovely clothes. Today she had on a new pair of cropped jeans, a black and white stripy tunic and a very nice denim jacket that went in at the waist and had little beads and sequins sewn onto the lapels and cuffs. Lynette's trainers were dazzlingly white. Caitlin felt quite scruffy beside her in her old jeans and hoodie. Caitlin sighed. She felt sad and a bit envious of all the time Lynette was able to spend with her mum, shopping for clothes and getting her hair done.

But Lynette's words pulled Caitlin back from such thoughts and she looked in the direction of the park gate. Sure enough there was Edward, with his trusty old duffle bag slung over his shoulder, biking along the path, past the no-cycling sign. She knew there was no point in waving, Edward wouldn't wave back. Not because he was being rude or stuck-up or anything. It was just one of the many things that Edward didn't or couldn't do. But besides that, waving would be tricky as he was riding his bike *and* carrying something.

Edward leant his bike against the bench where the girls had left theirs, and strolled over to join the girls.

There was a group of teenagers over on the grass, some sitting on the ground, and a couple of them leaning against a tree. They were laughing and shouting and the two leaning against the tree were smoking. Joggers and dog-walkers also passed through and there was an old lady and a man sitting on one of the benches and throwing bread for the pigeons. But apart from some mums and toddlers, they had the play area to themselves.

"New mapstick?" Lynette said. She was now doing bendy things with her knees, and using the swing frame as a ballet barre.

"Yep," Edward said.

"Did you have a good holiday?" Caitlin asked, letting the swing she was sitting on bob back and forward.

Edward gave a little nod. "Yep."

"The mapstick, is it stuff from America?" Lynette asked, practising the complete set of arm positions that ballet dancers use in their dances.

"Yep," Edward said again.

"So, tell us what's on it and how you made this one," Lynette said, as she waggled her arms.

"It's a baton. Mum and Dad took me to see an American

marching band. Some of the marchers twirl a baton like this one. I got it at a stall in the field where the band was marching. And it's not just a mapstick."

"What else is it?" Lynette asked.

"It's a complete diary stick for my holiday."

"Right," Lynette said, looking more closely at the stick. "What did you tie the stuff on with? It's not your usual wool, is it?"

"Ribbons —they were round the top of the baton. I took them off and tied them along the stick."

"Cool," Lynette said.

"And they're red, white and blue like the American flag. That's cool too," Caitlin said.

Edward pointed to each item on the stick in turn. "Down at the bottom there's my plane ticket and a map of Disneyland, and then above that there's a photo of our hotel, a menu from the pizzeria that I liked. The curled pieces of paper, there's one for each day of the holiday, and on them I've written a daily journal. Then there's my Disneyland pass and the information leaflet. And at the top there's Mickey Mouse."

"Oh, yes. He's cute," Lynette said, looking at the small figure. It was the kind you get for putting on the end of a pencil but Edward had fixed it to the top of the stick.

"Did you like it in America?" Caitlin asked.

"Yep," Edward said. "I saw Mickey and Donald and Goofy and Pluto and loads of others. It was awesome." He swung his duffel bag round and off his shoulder. He reached inside the bag. "And—I got Mickey's autograph." He showed the girls a signed photo of the Mouse. "There's other stuff too. I got some figures." He produced several models of Disney characters. There was a Buzz Lightyear, a Spiderman and a Captain America. "Oh, these are for you." He handed both girls a small parcel each.

"Cool," Lynette said, sitting down at last. She sat on the

swing next to Caitlin's. Edward sat on the third of three swings, still holding his mapstick and with his bag at his feet.

The girls unwrapped their presents.

"Wow!" Caitlin said. "Princess Merida! I love that film! Thanks, Ed." She held up the figure of the heroine from Brave.

"She sort of looks like you," Edward said ,"With her red hair."

"And I've got Cinderella in her ballgown," Lynette said, smiling. "Thanks so much."

"Well you like dancing and so did Cinderella so..."

"It makes sense, yes." Lynette smiled again.

"And you weren't frightened on the plane?" Caitlin asked.

"No, it was okay. My dad was allowed to take me to see the pilot before we took off and the pilot told me how the plane gets up in the air and how it stays there and then gets down again. I wrote it all down in my notebook so I could check that everything happened right."

"Good," Caitlin said. She'd been a bit concerned about her friend going all the way to America. He'd never flown before because he got too worried about going in a plane. Edward found new things very difficult. He liked things best if he knew all about them. There were some things he knew lots about, like Disney characters. He had loads of DVDs of Disney films and loads of Disney games and books and posters.

Sometimes, at school, he got upset if unexpected things happened, like if Miss Stewart was off sick or the class's P.E. time was changed without warning. Miss Stewart had a helper lady, Mrs Maxwell, and she would help to keep Edward calm when he got flustered, and she would explain things to Edward or take him for a walk in the school grounds if he got really upset. Caitlin also worried about how he'd get on at high school. Edward didn't speak much at school. He only really talked to Caitlin and Lynette. He hardly even spoke to Miss Stewart or Miss Maxwell. Some of the kids made fun of him because he was a bit different. Kids like Craig Wilmot and Corinna Grey, who didn't get that Edward had a thing called Asperger's, and it was part of him, and actually made him a really good pal. They called him a crybaby and a scaredy and said things to him like, 'you're not right in the head'.

Caitlin often wished the bullies could see Edward when he was horse-riding. He was never afraid or upset then. She and Edward both went riding most weekends. They were in the 'Be Happy on a Horse' riding club. The head teacher at their school had told them about it. She said it was for children who deserved a bit of a treat and who would benefit from being with horses. Caitlin had started going just after her mum died and Edward had started around the same time. They both loved it.

Edward began to swing. The girls laid their presents down on the grass and joined in. Legs out on the forward swoop then tucked back and pushing hard on the upswing.

Soon they were all soaring. *'Up in the air and down'* thought Caitlin, recalling the poem 'The Swing' by Robert Louis Stevenson that Miss Stewart had read to them last term.

"How do you like to go up in a swing, up in the air so blue?" she recited.

The other two joined in, matching the poem's rhythm to the pace of their swinging. "Oh, I do think it the pleasantest thing ever a child can do!" They all laughed.

"Aw, isn't that nice," came a voice. "Bizarre boy, Ginger Cat and the ballerina all having a laugh. What's so funny oddbods?" Craig Wilmot grinned at his companion, Corinna.

"None of your business," Lynette said. Both she and Caitlin had slowed their swinging but Edward kept going and didn't even look in Craig's direction.

"Oo, 'none of your business'," Corinna mocked.

The park seemed suddenly quiet and empty. Caitlin glanced around. The teenagers, the mums and small children, even the dog-walkers had all gone. She thought she saw someone over by the trees, but when she looked back a few seconds later, the person had gone.

"Oh, look, mad lad's got one of his sticks. What's this one all about? Taking it in to show the teachers when school starts?" Craig sneered.

Edward didn't respond, just kept swinging. But Craig didn't like being ignored. He stepped forward and grabbed the chains of Edward's swing, forcing it to stop, forcing Edward to look at him. Caitlin and Lynette glanced at each other. Both girls stood up. Corinna stepped in front of them. Caitlin pushed past her and Lynette darted round the long way. The girls stood either side of Edward.

"Oi!" shouted Corinna, trying and failing to grab Caitlin's sleeve. "Who do you think you're shoving? Craig tell her!"

But Craig wasn't listening. He was bent over, his face close to Edward's. "I said—"

"I heard you," Edward said, looking down at the ground. "Yep, I've got one of my mapsticks. It shows stuff I did in America. No, I'll not take it to school. You don't take this sort of stuff into high school." Edward stood up, forcing Craig to step back.

Craig made a grab for the mapstick. Edward tried to back away, but got tangled in the swing. Caitlin stepped in between Craig and Edward. Craig swiped at her, knocking her over. He made another grab for the stick. This time he got it. Caitlin staggered to her feet as Craig waved the stick just out of Edward's reach.

Craig was a head taller than all the others, but Lynette didn't let that put her off. She executed a perfect *grande jeté*, in an attempt to wrestle the mapstick from Craig's grasp. But Corinna moved quickly and grabbed her around the waist.

Corinna also managed to pin Lynette's arms to her sides so she couldn't try it again.

"Give it back," Caitlin shouted. Her face was red with fury and her hands were tight fists.

But Craig just laughed. "Oh, watch out, Ginger's going to lose that temper of hers. I'm really scared. You carrot-tops, when you lose it, you really lose it. Isn't that right?" Corinna's cackles joined Craig's snorts of laughter. Lynette struggled to free herself but Corinna was bigger and stronger. Edward, meanwhile, had sat back down on the swing and was looking at the ground.

Caitlin was so enraged, she ran and jumped on Craig's back and made wild swipes at the stick. This just made Craig laugh all the more, and he easily shook her off. All she could do was sit on the ground, as she had landed, and watch.

"Okay," Craig said, sneering and peering at the mapstick. "Let's see what we have here." He pulled the Mickey Mouse figure off the top of the mapstick and flung it onto the grass at the edge of the play area. "Bye, Mickey," he said. Then he ripped off, screwed up and threw away the remaining items. All this was accompanied by Corinna's cheers, as she continued to hold onto, a still struggling, Lynette. He finished off by snapping the stick in two and dropping it at his feet. "Oh dear," he said bending down, his head beside Edward's. "It looks like your stickie thing's had a wee bit of an accident."

Edward continued looking down at the ground. Caitlin felt cross with Edward. Why didn't he, just this once, defend himself? Of course she knew that wasn't Edward's way. Whenever he was in a situation he couldn't deal with, it was as if he just shut down, like a computer crashing. Caitlin realised this, but she still felt cross with him, even though she knew she shouldn't and that Edward didn't choose to be the way he was.

Craig shook his head when Edward didn't react. "God, you're such a wimp!"

"Get lost, Craig!" Caitlin shouted at the same time as Lynette kicked Corinna hard in the shin.

"Ow!" Corinna immediately letting go of Lynette. She hopped about and rubbed her leg. "She kicked me!" Corinna wailed at Craig. "She kicked me!"

"Yeah!" Craig laughed, "It was a good kick—for a girl."

"What?" Corrina yelped.

"Stop whining and see what's in the wimp's bag," Craig said.

"Oh yeah," Corinna grabbed the duffle bag and turned it upside down. She shook out the contents. "Dolls! Bizarre boy's got dolls!" She stamped on them one by one. "Oh and a photo of Mickey Mouse. Sweet!" She snatched it up and tore it in two, and the pieces fluttered to the grass.. Then she spotted Caitlin and Lynette's presents. She went to grab them.

But Caitlin, who was still sitting on the ground, lunged towards the two small figures and got to them before Corinna. She scooped them up and held them to her chest as she stood up. "Oh no you don't!" she said.

"Make her hand them over, Craig," Corinna said.

But Craig just shrugged. "Nah, I'm bored now," he said. "Let's go." And he walked off. Corinna stumbled after him. "I'll get you back, Lady Lynette and you, Carrot Top. I'll get you back!" she called over her shoulder.

"Whatever," Lynette said under her breath. She picked up some of the Disney characters and the pieces of the photo. She tried to rub the figures clean on her sweatshirt. They were muddy but not damaged. She returned them to the duffle bag and walked over to Edward with the torn up photo. "You'll be able to tape this back together." She held the pieces out to him but he wouldn't look at her, wouldn't take the ripped picture from her. She sighed and put the pieces in his bag. Then she sat back on the swing next to him.

Caitlin meanwhile had snatched up the broken stick and begun searching for the things Craig had torn off it. She knew it was probably pointless, but she didn't want the other two to see the angry tears that were running down her cheeks. *Poor, poor Edward,* she thought. *How could Craig be so horrible? And as for that Corinna, why did she hang about with him? He clearly didn't seem to like her much. He wasn't exactly sympathetic when she got kicked.*

She found the pizzeria menu torn in two, and the Disneyland map all scrunched up. The other bits of paper, including the diary entries had been torn up into such small bits, it was hard to tell if she'd got everything, but she did manage to retrieve Mickey from the grass.

She wiped her tears with her sleeve and made her way back to the other two. Both of them were sitting on the swings. Edward's head remained down and Lynette was looking at him, as if she believed that the power of her stare would force him to look up. She glanced at Caitlin as she approached and shook her head.

"I think I found everything," Caitlin said. She looked at Edward. He didn't look back. She knelt in front of him and held all the stuff she'd gathered in her hands. "Edward," she said softly.

He moved his head slightly. Caitlin knew he was looking at the sorry remains. He leaned forward and scooped them up into his hands. Then he stood up and dropped them at his feet and stamped on them. He almost kneed Caitlin in the face. Shocked, she backed away.

"I don't want them anymore!" he shouted. "Take them away!"

Lynette tried to grab his arm, to calm him down, but he shrugged her off. He strode away towards the bikes. Before the stunned girls could move, he'd got his cycle helmet on.

"Come on!" said Lynette, as Edward got on his bike. "We need to go after him."

Caitlin scooped up as many of the discarded bits as she could, before running after her friend.

Chapter Three

It didn't take the girls long to catch up with Edward. They'd guessed correctly that he'd be heading for home. They cycled up behind him just before he arrived at his house. Caitlin rang her bicycle bell and he glanced back over his shoulder. He didn't say anything, just kept on pedalling up to his gate.

"Edward, wait, please," Caitlin shouted as he got off his bike. He left it lying on the drive and headed straight for the front door. She abandoned her own bike at the gate and ran after him. "Edward, stop, please, stop. I've got Mickey. I picked him up."

Edward stopped. He turned to face Caitlin. "I don't want him. You have him." He looked miserable.

"But he's yours. You were so proud of him. Here—"

"I don't want him!" Edward shouted. He sounded really angry.

Lynette struggled up to them, wheeling both her own bike and Caitlin's. "Hey, Ed, don't shout at Caitlin. She's trying to make you feel better. We both tried to help, you know."

Edward looked down at his feet. "Sorry," he murmured and went to sit on the front step.

The girls joined him, one on either side. "Craig and Corinna, they're bullies, Ed," Caitlin said. She risked putting her hand on his arm as she spoke, even though she knew he didn't really like being touched. She so wanted to reassure him. "It was horrible what they did, and Lynette and me, we're really sad for you. I'm so angry that we couldn't stop them, but one day, one day—"

"I know," Edward said. "I know you tried to stop them." He nudged Caitlin's hand off his arm. "And thank you for trying. But it doesn't matter. The stick's broken and that's that. My father's right. I need to toughen up. I'm a coward. I don't know how to fight."

"Not being able to fight doesn't make you a coward, Ed," Caitlin said.

"It does according to my father." Edward looked so sad that Caitlin felt she might cry again. She risked patting Edward on the arm for a second time.

He stood up. "I'm okay," he said.

"So, what now?" Lynette asked.

Caitlin glanced at her watch. It was half-past twelve. "I better get back for lunch," she said. She realised she hadn't had the chance to tell the other two about Scary Lady yet and she really needed to share. "But we could meet up again this afternoon. What about the Hermitage, about two-fifteen at the gate?"

"Yeah," Lynette said. "Gran's at mine while Mum's at work. She'll be making some lunch, but she'll be quite happy for me to be out from under her feet again this afternoon."

"Yep," Edward said. "I'll be there."

As he spoke, they heard Edward's mother calling. "Edward, is that you?"

"Don't tell," Edward whispered, as the front door opened behind them. The three of them jumped to their feet.

Mrs Farquharson was very protective of Edward and she trusted Caitlin to look out for him. It was only recently that he'd been allowed out at all without his mother accompanying him. If Edward's mother knew what had happened at the park, he wouldn't be allowed out on his own again for a very long time.

"Ah, good, you're back, darling," Mrs Farquharson said.

"Hello, girls."

"Hello, Mrs Farquharson," Caitlin said. "How are you? Did you and Mr Farquharson enjoy your holiday?"

"Yes we had a lovely time. We felt like children again ourselves. It was great fun."

"That's good," Caitlin said.

Mrs Farquharson peered all around. "Edward, didn't you take your holiday mapstick with you to show the girls? You said you were going to."

Edward looked at the ground.

"Yeah," Lynette said. "He did say he was going to bring it, but he must have forgotten. We can see it later."

Caitlin looked at the ground too. She was always amazed at how quick-thinking Lynette was. She never seemed to panic and told lies awesomely.

Mrs Farquharson smiled at Lynette. She also glanced at the duffle bag. "And did you give the girls their presents and show them all the other bits and pieces you got?"

"Yes I did," Edward replied.

"Good," his mother said. "Right, come on then, lunch is ready."

After the front door had closed behind Edward and his mother, the girls picked up their bikes and walked to the gate.

"Well done, not saying what really happened to the stick, or the other stuff," Caitlin said, as she and Lynette put their cycle helmets back on. "I hoped we wouldn't have to mention it at all."

"Yeah, trust Mrs F. She doesn't miss much, does she? But I knew it would be a hundred years before poor Ed would be allowed out of her sight again. Can you imagine what it would be like if she knew about Craig and the bullying?"

"I know," said Caitlin. "And I know Edward didn't want us to mention it. But..."

"But, what?"

"But, you know, how Miss Stewart said, when we did the Stamp Out Bullying thing, she said you should always tell an adult if someone's bullying you, or someone else you know. Maybe we should have said."

"Yeah, and we will, if we have to, if we can't handle it, or if Edward can't. But his mother will be impossible if we do. Edward would have no life. He'd have to sit at home with Mummy all the time. And he'd have to listen to his dad going on about him being a coward."

"Poor Edward," Caitlin said. "I suppose his dad just wants him to stick up for himself. I'm sure he doesn't want Ed to get hurt. And it's sort of a shame for Mrs Farquharson too." Caitlin remembered Dad being cross once with her big sister, Fiona, for saying Edward's mum was a snob. "Dad says she's like she is because Edward's got Asperger's. It must make her worried and want to protect him."

"Yes, well, all the more reason not to worry her, then. It's not fair if Edward has to suffer all the more. His Asperger's shouldn't mean he can't have a life. Anyway, I'm going to come up with a plan to take care of Craig and Corinna once and for all."

"Oh, what's your plan?"

"I said I'm going to come up with one. I haven't got one yet!" Lynette laughed.

"And if you do, and it doesn't work, or if you don't come up with anything, we'll tell, yeah?"

Lynette nodded. "Deal," she said, getting on her bike. "See you at the Hermitage later."

The girls prepared to set off in opposite directions.

"Oh, I nearly forgot," Lynette called over her shoulder. "What's your new childminder like?"

"Later," Caitlin replied. She waved and pedalled away.

It was quarter-past-one when Caitlin scraped to a stop on the gravel drive outside her house. She knew she was late but only by fifteen minutes and Bella hadn't texted her to find out where she was. She hoped that meant she wasn't in trouble.

A wonderful aroma greeted her when she let herself into the house. It smelled like Granny's house when she'd been baking. Caitlin went straight to the kitchen.

Sure enough, there on the worktop was a batch of muffins and beside them a cake, a sponge cake with white icing and sprinkles. Bella was at the table eating a sandwich and drinking tea from her china cup. The snowstorm ornament was also on the table.

"Hello," Bella said, smiling her sparkly smile. "Did you have a nice morning with your friends?"

"Yes," Caitlin said. She felt a bit awkward, unsure if she was in trouble.

"Nothing happened that worried you?"

Caitlin was startled by the question. She remembered the feeling she'd had at the park, the feeling someone was watching. But it couldn't have been Bella. Could it? Why would she? "No!" she replied.

"Good. Come on then, sit down. I'll get your sandwiches. I started without you. Like I said, lunch was to be at one o'clock and everything was ready so..." Bella opened the fridge.

"Yeah, I'm sorry—"

"No, no it's all right," Bella said, bringing a plate of sandwiches and a glass of milk over to the table. "Don't apologise. I know you had things to sort out."

Caitlin sat down and stared at Bella's back. How did Bella know? Bella pointed at Caitlin's plate, "Cheese and pickle," she said. "Tuck in."

"Thanks ," Caitlin said and began eating the best cheese and pickle sandwiches she'd ever tasted.

"And Edward is okay?" asked Bella

Caitlin nearly choked on her sandwich. What did Bella know? How did she know? How did she even know Edward's name? But all she said was, "Yeah, he's okay."

"That's good." Bella poured herself another cup of tea.

"I really am sorry I was late," Caitlin said. "I hope you weren't worried."

"No," Bella replied. "I knew you were all right, and that you'd be home just as soon as you'd done what you needed to do."

"How did you know?"Caitlin asked.

Bella glanced at the snowstorm ornament. "Ah, now, that's a long story," she said. "But now's not the time for you to hear it."

Chapter Four

A little while later, Caitlin was standing beside her bike at the gate to the Hermitage of Braid, watching Edward and Lynette cycling towards her. Lots of little birds flitted and chirped in the trees round about her. A goldfinch landed right beside her on the wall. She thought goldfinches were probably her favourite little birds with their gorgeous scarlet and yellow feathers. It had something in its beak – a piece of red, striped material. The colourful little bird cocked its head and seemed to look her in the eye, as if checking her out.

"So, what do you want to do?" Caitlin asked, when the other two joined her.

"Climb up the hill," Edward said. "I'm going to make a new mapstick – for here. So I want to collect stuff along the way."

"Cool," Lynette said. "Let's walk the bikes along to the Visitor Centre and padlock them at the bike stands. Then we can get climbing. And, when we're at the top, Caitlin can tell us all about her new childminder."

Edward nodded and he and Lynette set off.

"You okay?" Lynette called, looking back at Caitlin who hadn't moved.

"Yeah," Caitlin said, forcing a smile. "I'm just coming!" She felt torn. Part of her wanted to share the momentous news about Bella, and part of her was scared of how they might react.

"Oh, I like your backpack. It's really neat. Is it new?" Lynette said as Caitlin caught up to them.

Caitlin smiled and glanced down over her shoulder. "I bought it on holiday in Skye," she said, pleased Lynette liked it. She only had her purse and phone in it and had really only brought it to show it off to her friends. She'd bought it at the visitor centre in Portree the week before. Dad had taken her there to watch sea eagles on a webcam. He got very excited when he saw one of the enormous white-tailed birds. They were quite an impressive sight, but she'd actually preferred the shop. The backpack was small, school-bag sized. "It's Cameron tartan."

"It's lovely!" Lynette said. "Isn't it, Ed?"

"Mmm," Edward said. He didn't look all that impressed. But that was okay. He was a boy after all.

"Oh, and I got something for both of you," Caitlin said. She unhooked the carrier bag that was dangling from the handlebars of her bike. She reached in and then passed them a small parcel each. "I hope you like them," she said, as she watched her friends unwrap their presents.

"Cool!" Lynette said when she discovered her present was a purse. "Thank you." She hugged Caitlin.

"You're welcome," Caitlin said. "It's Maclean tartan. And there's a pound coin inside. Granny said I should put one in to bring you good luck."

"Oh, so there is," Lynette said. "Thank you so much. I love it." She hugged Caitlin again and then popped the purse in the pocket of her jeans. "So this tartan stuff— your Cameron one and this Maclean one—there's a tartan for each family name, is there?"

"Sort of, I think so, but only in Scotland, of course."

"Not all family names have tartans to go with them," Edward said. "It's mainly Highland families, and they're sort of grouped together into clans, like big tribes. It's the clans who have their own tartans."

"How do you know all that?" Lynette asked, shaking her head.

Caitlin laughed. "I don't believe it. He's started reading his present already. Dad said he'd probably like it because it's so full of facts." She pointed at the book Edward held in his hand. "It's called 'The Young Person's Guide to the Highland Clans of Scotland'."

"Ah," Lynette said, smiling. "And you'd read all you just said, just now, walking along, bike in one hand, book in the other?"

"Yep, while you two were doing all that hugging stuff." He raised the book in one hand, before dropping it into the empty carrier bag he'd produced from his pocket. "Thanks Caitlin. It looks really interesting."

To get to the Visitor Centre, they had to walk about a kilometre along the side of the Braid Burn. The shallow but fast-flowing stream ran right through the Hermitage. They passed the wildflower meadow where Miss Stewart had brought them to sketch the wood sorrel flowers just before the holidays. Miss Stewart often brought the class here for lessons on nature and on ecology. And then it was on past the dovecot which stood on the other side of the burn.

They stopped for a moment at the weir. Caitlin remembered Miss Stewart telling the class that the weir had been built to give water power to the mill that had been there long ago. She wondered if that fact would qualify as history and if Bella would be impressed that she knew it. A goldfinch landed at Caitlin's feet. It chirped and looked up at her. She thought it might be the same bird that she'd seen at the gate.

The path was bumpy with the roots of the many trees that lined it. Caitlin and Lynette could only remember the names of some of them from Miss Stewart's lessons, from when they'd done bark and leaf rubbings, but Edward could name them all. He pointed out ash, elm, sycamore, rowan, birch, oak, pine and horse chestnut. He gathered a few of the leaves from several of the trees and put them in his carrier bag. He also spotted a small branch about half a metre long that had fallen from one of the pine trees. It had lost most of its needles. He'd snatched it up. "This will be my new stick," he said. "It's just right and look, it's already got something stuck to it."

The girls looked. Sure enough there was a scrap of red, striped material skewered onto one of the remaining pine needles.

"I'll take that as well," Edward said, picking up a small, bright red and yellow feather that lay beside where the branch had been.

Lining the path's edge were bluebells and little pink flowers that Edward remembered were called campion. He picked a few of these too and added them to his leaf collection. Caitlin was almost certain you weren't supposed to pick wild flowers, but she didn't have the heart to tell Edward off and he only took a few. And again she noticed the loud chirping of the birds. It reminded her of the dinner hall noise at school with everyone chatting at once. Two blue tits hopped across the path in front of them and a tiny wren peeped out from under a bush.

Soon they arrived at the Visitor Centre and left their bikes padlocked to the cycle rack then walked back up to the main path.

They reached the ice house on the right of the path just above the Centre and stopped to look inside. It was the place where ice had been stored long ago, when the Visitor Centre had been a big mansion house that a rich family had lived in, in the days before fridges were invented. The cook, or somebody like that, would have bought the ice to put in the ice house, and then meat and stuff could be stored there in the cold and dark.

"It's such a cool wee place," Lynette said, laughing. "Do you get it? A *cool* wee place!"

"Yeah," Caitlin said . "Very funny."

Edward looked puzzled for a moment and then he nodded. "Oh, I see. Cool and ice. It was a joke." He nodded again, muttering to himself, "Cool—ice—cool. Good, yes I see."

Lynette shook her head and giggled. "Oh, Ed you're so funny sometimes!"

"Am I?" Edward asked, as he bent to pick up what looked like a half-chewed pine cone. He put it into his plastic bag.

After they crossed the Scout Bridge, it wasn't far to the foot of Blackford hill. Going up this side of the hill, was a very steep climb, and they were all out of breath by the time they got to the radio mast at the top. They found a nice flat rock to sit on and get their breath back and could see practically the whole of Edinburgh. There was the castle, the parliament building, and another hill, called Arthur's Seat, which was the shape of a crouching lion. They could also see Waverley train station and Princes Street and in the distance the River Forth shone like a blue satin ribbon.

Edward took some green wool out of his pocket. He used it to tie a label to his new mapstick.

Caitlin glanced at the label. Edward had obviously prepared it before he'd left home. It had the date and Hermitage of Braid printed on it. It also had Edward's name on it, along with her own and Lynette's. "Are you going to tie the leaves and flowers you collected onto the stick?" Caitlin asked.

"No, they'll wither and die quite quickly, so I'll sketch them and then cut out the sketches and attach them. But I'll put the pine cone on."

"But it's half-eaten!" Lynette said.

"Yes, exactly. That shows there are squirrels here."

"Why do you like making the sticks so much?" Lynette asked.

Edward sighed. "I've told you before. It was used long ago by tribes on islands in the Pacific as a way of making hunting maps. I like it because it's a way of recording stuff without doing lots of writing. So after this walk today, I'll have a stick that will show where we walked, what we saw and in the order they happened. I'll use blue wool to represent the burn, and wind it along the stick. And I'll use grey wool to stand for the path. Then there are the birds. There'll be red and yellow wool for the goldfinches we saw and so on like that. It's more interesting than a diary and anyone can understand it. You don't even have to be able to read."

Lynette nodded. "Yeah, I can see that."

The children stared out at the city

"I'm thirsty," Lynette said.

"I'd like something to eat," Edward said.

"Yeah, we should have brought stuff with us," Caitlin said. She decided to take some photos of the view and unzipped her backpack to get her phone out. But there was something else in the bag, besides her purse and her phone. She brought out a tinfoil package and then three small cartons of apple juice—the ones with the little straws attached.

"Oh, you were teasing!" Lynette said. "You did bring drinks. And what's in there?"

"I don't know," Caitlin said, pulling back the foil.

"Three bits of cake!" Lynette said. "I love icing and sprinkles! You are so clever."

Edward leaned over to look at the cake. He smiled his Edward smile. "Mmm," he said.

Caitlin just about managed to smile. She didn't know how to start explaining. Bella must have put the stuff in her backpack. But how had she known that she would take the bag, and when had she done it? Her bag had been up in her room while she ate lunch. The cake was whole when she arrived in the kitchen, and Bella hadn't left the kitchen at all.

Caitlin was still trying to figure out how Bella had done it when Lynette said, through a mouthful of cake, "So, the new childminder, who is she? What's she like?"

"Scary Lady," Caitlin said, feeling her face go hot. Edward froze, his piece of cake halfway to his mouth. He stared at Caitlin.

"The childminder's *like* Scary Lady?" Lynette said, before taking a swig of juice.

Edward shook his head. "No, Caitlin means she *is* Scary Lady!"

Lynette choked on her drink.

Caitlin looked at Edward. He'd understood straight away.

"Yeah, right," said Lynette. "Seriously, is she nice? Is she cool like Susie was?"

"Ed's right. It *is* her. It's the woman we call Scary, the strange lady that we see in the street and at the shops. The one with the long purple coat and the hat with the earflaps, the one who talks to herself. Her name is Bella Blawearie, and the place that finds people to look after children sent her to fill in until they get a replacement for Susie. And no, she's nothing like Susie." Caitlin bit her lip. This was so embarrassing. What if Craig or Corinna found out? She couldn't bear to think about that.

"Okay," Lynette said. "Okay." She took another bite of cake and seemed to be thinking as she chewed.

Caitlin wished she would speak, tell her it was kind of cool, tell her it would be all right, they'd soon be back at school, and she'd soon have a proper minder.

"Did she make this cake?" Edward asked

"Yes, she did," Caitlin said.

"So she must be a kind person," Edward said. "If you make a cake and then you share it, that's a kind thing to do, isn't it?"

Caitlin shrugged. She'd thought it was Bella's way of trying to trick her into liking her. Like the new girl that came into their class last term and kept giving people presents to try to get them to be her friend. "I don't really know what she's like. I only met her this morning. All she's done so far is make breakfast and lunch for me."

"And cake," Edward said.

"Yes, and cake," Caitlin agreed.

"She sounds all right to me," Edward said.

At last Lynette spoke. "But she's really old. And that coat. And what does she know about looking after kids? Does she know what to do?"

"She must know how to look after children," Edward said. He flattened his empty juice carton, and folded the foil that had been wrapped around the cake as he spoke. "My mum told me that people who work with children have to pass some sort of test and get a certificate that says they can be trusted. Mum said she checked that the Sunday school teacher, and the cub leader, and the man who takes the scouts, all had their certificates before she let any of them near me."

"What sort of things do the certificate givers check?" Lynette asked, as she handed Edward her empty carton for squashing.

"I don't know exactly. Probably stuff like does the person know how to stop kids from setting fire to themselves, or poking each other's eyes out, and how to put on plasters or get an ambulance, and, probably, how to get kids to behave without shouting at them. You know—respect us and stuff." As he finished speaking, Edward picked up Caitlin's discarded carton and flattened it like the other two.

"So, is old Bella scary? Like when you see her in Sainsbury's talking away to herself?" Lynette asked.

"No, not scary exactly. And she's not really old—not like our grandparents, anyway. She's more like my dad or your mum—their kind of old. Her hair is bright red and today she's wearing a really short kilt and biker boots and she's got big hoop earrings."

"You're kidding!" Lynette said.

"No, it's true," Caitlin said. "When you really look at her, and especially when she takes that stupid coat off, she's not at all what you expect."

"Maybe the coat makes her feel safe," Edward said. "But underneath she's not weird at all."

"Hmm," Caitlin said, not sure what he meant. She decided not to mention about the cup and saucer thing, or the history thing, or that she suspected Bella was also a mind reader—not yet anyway. She'd had enough of talking about Bella. She took her phone out of her bag and stood up. "Right," she said. "I'm going to take some photos."

While Caitlin took pictures of the city below them, Edward got rid of their litter in the bin over by the radio mast, and Lynette did some pirouettes and arabesques. When Caitlin had all the shots she wanted, she rejoined the other two.

"Let's see your pictures," Lynette said.

"Did you take any on Skye?" Edward asked.

"Yes, I did," Caitlin said. "I'll show you."

Caitlin showed her friends the photos she'd just taken and then she scrolled back to the ones she'd taken on Skye.

"What's that?" Lynette asked, when they came to the picture of the locket.

"That's the silver locket. Granny gave it to me to keep. It's made of real silver and it's been in my family for a very long time. It's nearly three hundred years old, so I've not to take it out the house until I'm older. Granny says it belonged to her ancestor, Flora Macdonald."

"What? Flora Macdonald that rescued Bonnie Prince Charlie?" Edward asked.

"Yes, that's right. It was the Prince who gave her the locket," Caitlin said. "You know about him, do you, Ed?"

"Yes, I do. I read about it. It's an interesting story. The Jacobites, they had a rebellion in 1745 and a battle against England a year later because they wanted Prince Charlie to be king. And you have a real piece of that," Edward said.

"That's good."

"I suppose so, yes," Caitlin said.

"Boring!" Lynette said. "I mean, it's a lovely locket and all, and I want to see it next time I'm at your house, but I can't be bothered with all that old history stuff." She stood up. "What will we do now?"

"Let's go over to the Observatory," Edward said, already starting to walk off in that direction. The girls followed him.

They walked across the top of the hill and down the sloping path to the Royal Observatory. Caitlin's dad had brought her to visit the Observatory on several occasions and more recently her big sister, Fiona, had taken her. It was best to come at night, and then you could look through the huge telescopes at the planets and the millions of stars and the universe.

Fiona wanted to be an astronaut when she left university. She'd been to the Scottish Space School to stay for a week in the summer holidays before she left high school. She got to do lots of science stuff and meet real astronauts who'd been into space. And that was when she decided. Now she was at university she was learning more about science and the planets and everything, and she knew the names of lots of the groups of stars. Fiona's eyes went all shiny when she spoke about space, and Caitlin liked to listen to her. Caitlin thought she might be an astronaut too, although she also wanted to be a teacher, like Miss Stewart, or maybe a doctor like her dad.

"Look," Edward said, stopping and pointing at the cloudless sky, as they approached the Observatory car park. The girls stopped and looked up. Overhead a bird circled and hovered. "A kestrel," he said. "He'll be watching for a mouse."

"Aw, poor wee mouse! Shoo, nasty bird!" Lynette flapped her arms above her head. The kestrel stayed where it was.

Edward frowned at Lynette and then looked back at the bird. Caitlin laughed.

"What?" Lynette said.

"The kestrel has to eat. It can't go to Tesco and buy its tea."

"But mice are so cute. It's a shame to kill them."

"So it's all right to eat things that aren't cute? Do you only eat ugly food? I don't think so. You eat little lambs and wee pigs and cute chickens and nobody comes and shoos you away," Edward said.

Lynette opened her mouth, closed it again and then said, "That's different."

Edward just shook his head and watched as the kestrel flapped its wings and disappeared over to the other side of the hill.

"Okay," Caitlin said. "Shall we go along by the golf course and head down into the wood? That'll take us back to the path."

"Yep," Edward said.

"Okay," Lynette said. She stood with her feet and arms in fifth position before doing three spins, and then she skipped gracefully along the path in front of the other two.

The small, community wood was cool and shady and they stopped for a few moments to watch some grey squirrels scampering up and down the trees and round and round the base of the trunks. When they came out at the other side of the wood there were some steps to go down and this took them back onto the path.

Here the path was much more open than it was at the start of the walk. There were fewer trees and the grass on the other side of the burn was covered in little pink flowers, which of course Edward knew the name of.

"Rosebay willowherb," he said. He reached into his pocket and produced a small notebook and a pencil. The notebook and pencil went everywhere with him and he often stopped whatever he was doing to take notes. "I think I'll draw the willowherb in here. I haven't got it in any of my notebooks and I want to record seeing the kestrel too. He sat down on the grass at the water's edge and proceeded to write and sketch.

Lynette picked some daisies and then sat down to make a daisy chain. Caitlin decided to take more photos.

As she got her phone out of her bag, she had that feeling again. The same as in the morning at the park, as if she was being watched. Out of the corner of her eye she thought she saw something moving on the other side of the burn.

She went to the water's edge and sure enough, there was something standing in the long grass on the far bank. She peered at the grey shape. It was a bird, long and skinny, with a big beak and it was statue-still, peering into the water.

"What's that?" she whispered to Edward and pointed at the bird.

"A heron," Edward whispered back. "It'll be waiting for a fish to come along." He glanced over at Lynette who was still fastening daisies together. "But don't tell Lynette. She probably thinks fish are cute as well."

Caitlin giggled and raised her phone and took a picture of the heron. Then she took one of Lynette wearing her daisy-chain necklace, and one of Edward with his notebook and carrier bag. Edward meanwhile quickly sketched the heron and a couple of daisies.

It was almost half-past-four when they passed by the ice house and turned onto the path to the Visitor Centre. They went straight over to the cycle rack and then just stared in disbelief. Their bikes were gone.

Chapter Five

It was all quite exciting, after the shock wore off. Edward got a bit panicky but the girls were able to calm him down. The lady in the Visitor Centre called the police and Caitlin called her dad. Caitlin's father had just arrived home and said he'd come and fetch all three of them in the car. He also said he'd let Edward's mum know. Caitlin was glad about that because she knew her dad would help Edward's mum not to worry. Lynette used Caitlin's phone to call her gran. Caitlin's dad arrived at the same time as the police.

The policeman and the policewoman asked them lots of questions about what time they'd left their bikes and what make and colour their bikes were. Edward was able to answer all these questions, including the makes of the girls' bikes. The officers also asked them if they'd seen anyone hanging about the cycle rack when they'd locked up their bikes. They said they hadn't.

The policeman found their padlocks and chains in the long grass at the side of the Centre. The chains had been cut through, and the bikes, with the helmets still attached to the handlebars, had been taken away.

The lady at the Centre said she hadn't seen anything, that there hadn't been any other bike thefts recently, and, no, they didn't have a security camera.

The policewoman wrote down everything they said, and told them the police would let them know if their bikes were found.

By the time they'd dropped off Lynette and Edward, it was after six o'clock when Caitlin and her dad got home. Bella was still there. She was sitting at the kitchen table, typing something on a tablet computer. Jack Russell was asleep on her lap. The little dog opened one eye and raised an ear as they walked in.

"Miss Blawearie," Dad said, laying his car keys and phone on the worktop by the kitchen door.

"Bella, please," she said, smiling at Dad.

Dad gave a little nod and, it seemed to Caitlin, he took a deep breath before saying, "Bella, yes, Bella." Then he just stood there looking daft and fiddling with his tie. Caitlin wondered why he was making such a big deal of saying her name. After all he'd always just called Susie —*Susie*, and not Miss Maxwell. And he'd never sounded nervous with Susie either.

While Caitlin stood pondering the strangeness of grown-ups, Jack stretched and jumped down. He walked over to Caitlin, sat at her feet and raised his paw, just as he'd done earlier. Caitlin crouched down and stroked him. He wagged his tail.

"So," Dad said to Bella, "What are you still doing here? I said there was no need to wait."

"I know you did. But Fiona and James arrived home just after you left and we got talking. What interesting young people your children are, Doctor Cameron! Anyway they said they were starving, so I thought I could organise some dinner for you all.

"You've cooked?" Dad said, looking over at the cooker. "There was really no need to do that."

Bella laughed. "No, I just looked at the menu for the Chinese takeaway." She turned the tablet round so dad could see the screen. "Fiona and James chose what they wanted before they disappeared upstairs. So, if you and Caitlin tell me what you'd like, I'll put in the order and then be on my way."

Caitlin had never had a Chinese takeaway before, and wasn't sure she'd even like it, but for some reason her mouth was watering.

"Oh, we don't—that is—the children—"

"Fiona and James told me you don't normally get takeaway food, but that they have it in term time when they're away at university. They were very keen—"

"I'm sure they were. But I don't happen to think takeaway food is either healthy or nutritious. My wife always cooked proper meals and I've tried to keep that up," Dad said.

Caitlin kept on stroking Jack. She thought her father sounded a bit cross. His voice had changed from the soppy one of a few minutes before when he'd said Bella's name. Now he was using that 'trying to be patient' voice that he sometimes used with her.

"And that is admirable. But surely the occasional indulgence won't do them any harm. I just thought that after Caitlin having her bike stolen, it would be a nice treat for everyone."

"I appreciate your thoughtfulness, but—"

"Have you ordered yet?" James said as he came into the kitchen. "I'm starving."

Fiona was right behind him. "Great idea, Dad—to get Chinese."

"What? I didn't—"

"Oh, don't say you haven't ordered yet? Come on what's the hold up? And yeah, I think it's cool too, Dad. At last, we're no longer a takeaway-free zone." James slapped Dad on the back. He glanced at the tablet screen. "So what'll it be?"

Bella picked up the tablet. "James, I don't think your father—

"No, I don't—know what to have," Dad said. He took the computer from Bella. "Caitlin, come and see and we'll decide." He sat down at the table opposite Bella and put his arm out to Caitlin. She went and stood beside him. "And, Bella, would you—that is—if you've no other plans—would you like to join us?"

An hour later they were all seated round the kitchen table. Caitlin had watched, amazed, as Dad and James unpacked all the foil cartons that had just been delivered.

Bella and Fiona took off the lids, and soon all the food was lined up down the centre of the table.

While they'd been waiting for the food to arrive, Dad had chopped up some ham from thr fridge for Jack. And so he'd been fed and was now curled up in the corner, snoozing on an old doll's blanket that Caitlin had found for him.

Caitlin loved the sweet and sour chicken with fried rice that Dad had suggested she might like. She couldn't eat all of it, but she did manage to taste some of Dad's beef chow mein and Fiona's lemon chicken. She liked both and she enjoyed the prawn crackers too.

Caitlin also enjoyed having everyone together at the table. It hardly ever happened anymore, now that Fiona and James were away during term time.

Dad and James were talking about some music that James had written. James was studying music at university and he could play the fiddle, the guitar and the bagpipes really well. And Fiona and Bella seemed to be talking about time or something. Caitlin couldn't really understand what the two of them were on about. But that didn't matter. It just felt really good to have their company. She didn't even mind that Bella was there.

She remembered how Susie used to make her dinner for her before Dad got home from the surgery. Sometimes Susie ate with her, but most times she just tidied up the kitchen while Caitlin ate on her own. But having everyone here like this was much nicer. And it helped her not to think about her bike. At least it did some of the time. Whenever it popped back into her head she got a sort of pain in her tummy. She didn't like to think of her bike being with somebody else. And she knew Edward was upset. He hadn't said much but she knew. She sighed.

"You okay, Caiti Maiti?" Dad put his hand on her arm.

Caitlin shook her head. "Not really. Do you think the police will get our bikes back?"

Dad raised his eyebrows. "I don't know. I'm sure they'll do their best."

"Edward will be really sad," Caitlin said. "Me and Lynette are sad too, but we can sort of understand it better. But Ed, he doesn't like unexpected stuff and he loved his bike. He knew the number on the frame off by heart and he had all his little Disney spoke decorators on the wheels. He had to send to America for them."

Dad leaned round from his seat at the end of the table and put his arm round Caitlin's shoulders. He kissed the top of her head. "Yes, it's upsetting—for Edward and for you and Lynette. But unfortunately these things happen, sweetheart. Try not to worry, okay?"

Caitlin nodded at her father and tried to smile. Why did horrible things have to happen? She glanced round the table. Everyone seemed to have finished eating. James was texting and Fiona also had her phone in her hand and was grinning away as she read something on the screen.

Bella was gathering up plates and cutlery. "Right," she said. "Who'd like some ice cream?"

"Cool!" James said, without looking up.

"Yes please," Fiona said.

"Do we have ice cream?" Dad asked.

"I got some earlier," Bella said. "I couldn't believe you didn't have any. Every house should have ice cream in case of emergencies."

"Oh," Dad said. And Caitlin was amazed when he laughed.

Bella went to the freezer. "Fiona, could you fetch some

bowls and a large spoon?" she said, as she carried the biggest ice cream tub Caitlin had ever seen to the table. "Now, while it softens a bit, James, you could clear all these plates over to the sink and take the containers to the bin."

"What?" James said, looking at Bella as if she'd spoken in Chinese, rather than just eaten the food.

Bella spoke slowly."Could you clear the table, please?"

"Oh, right, yeah," James said, continuing to text.

"Now, would be good," Bella said.

"Yes, right." James put his phone in his pocket and began to take the plates, one at a time, over to the worktop.

Bella shook her head. Even Caitlin knew that it would make more sense to pile the plates up.

Dad laughed and said, "It is his first time!" He got up to give James a hand. "I'll show you how it's done."

Fiona brought the pudding bowls to the table and sat down. "Poor Caiti," she said. "Such a shame about your bike. It's a pity you can't go back in time and stop it happening. Bella and I were just talking about time travel."

Caitlin looked across the table at Bella and Fiona. "What do you mean?"

"You know, like Dr Who does, being able to go back to last week, or hundreds of years, or to go into the future even, to the year 3000, or any time."

"Yes, but that's just pretend. The Tardis isn't real."

"I do know that!" Fiona said. "But at the university, we've been learning about how, one day, it might be possible in real life. Lots of physicists think it's perfectly possible. It's very much just a theory at the moment, but one day, one day, maybe, when I'm an astronaut..." Fiona went off into one of her daydreams.

Caitlin still wasn't sure what a physicist was. Whenever Fiona tried to explain she got all excited, like just now, and then went off somewhere in her own head. Caitlin wasn't sure what 'in theory' meant either, but she liked how happy

Fiona always looked when she talked about science stuff.

Bella cleared her throat. "But as I was saying to Fiona, perhaps travelling back and forward in time is already happening, perhaps it's always happened, but the scientists just don't know about it."

Fiona grinned as she spoke to Caitlin. "Yeah, and if it was possible we could send you back to earlier today and you would know not to take your bike out, or you could take it, but phone the police before it gets stolen."

"Yes!" said Caitlin. "We could go to the Hermitage and hide, and watch for the robbers and have the police arrest them when they were actually trying to steal our bikes."

"Ah, but then this evening wouldn't have happened, not like this," James said, as he and Dad rejoined the others at the table.

"What do you mean?" Caitlin asked.

"Dad wouldn't have had to go and get you. Bella would have gone home. Dad would have got dinner. No Chinese. So we wouldn't have this conversation. And I wouldn't have had to do all the clearing up."

Everyone laughed.

Caitlin thought she understood what James had just said. "So it's like there's a big plan and people can't go back and change things because that would spoil the plan?"

"Yes, exactly," James said.

"Well, unless…" Bella said, as she dished up the ice cream. "That is, it could be, perhaps the plan says that you must go back to *safeguard* the future."

"Nah." James shook his head. "There's no way that could, or should, be possible. What's past is past."

"I imagine it could be a dangerous thing to do," Dad said. "After all you might cause an accident or do something that results in your own ancestors not being born, and so you wouldn't be born either."

"And then," James said, waving his ice cream spoon in the

air as he spoke, "You couldn't go back in time because you wouldn't exist. But if you didn't go back and you didn't kill your ancestor then you would be born, so you'd be able to go back, and on and on in a loop. Chaos! No way does time travel happen. And it never will."

Caitlin tried her best to follow all this stuff about time travel. As she pondered, she ate her ice cream, which was a gorgeous, swirly, chocolate and vanilla mix.

"So," Fiona said to her brother, "You think life is all planned out, can't be changed and that everything that happens is meant to be?"

"No, no I think we can change things in the here and now, and that there's lots of possible lives for us all. I just know nobody can move backwards and forwards through time. Yesterday is gone and tomorrow hasn't happened yet." James gave his spoon a last lick and dropped it into his, now, empty bowl. He looked very pleased with himself, as if he had won the debate.

"I disagree," Bella said. "I think time is a river, not a conveyor belt, and it's a river full of life at all points along its course and the water swirls and circles as it flows." She, too, laid down her spoon in her empty bowl. And then, it seemed to Caitlin, that Bella was talking directly to her, rather than James. "And some of us get to navigate up and down that river."

Chapter Six

"I don't get it," Lynette said as she did some pas-de-chats. "I agree with James. You can't turn time backwards or forwards."

"Hmm," Caitlin sighed. "I'd like to just go with that too. And I don't really want to agree with Bella, but Fiona seems to believe what she says, and she even thinks she'll travel through time one day when she's an astronaut."

"I wouldn't like what Bella says to be true," Edward said. "It would be scary. Timetables wouldn't work if people were always going back and changing things. No, I'm with James."

It was the morning after the theft of their bikes and the three of them were in Lynette's bedroom.

Edward was sitting on the chair at Lynette's desk and Caitlin was sitting cross-legged on the bed. Lynette, of course, couldn't sit still and twirled, jumped and posed as they chatted. Caitlin had been telling her friends about the time travel conversation from the evening before.

"Anyway, never mind all that time stuff," Lynette said, plonking herself down at the end of the bed. "What's the plan for this afternoon? Time travel or no time travel, I think we should do a stakeout at the Hermitage."

"I'm not sure that's a good idea," Caitlin said.

"But you said you suggested it last night, a stakeout with the police on standby."

"Yes, but that was because of Bella's suggestion of being able to go back in time and prevent it happening in the first place."

Lynette wasn't put off. "Yeah, yeah, but it's still a good idea. I know the police won't come along, but at least we could set up the robbers and watch for them coming, film them on your phone and then give the evidence to the police."

"Don't you think we should leave it to the police to find the thieves?" said Caitlin.

"No, I don't!" said Lynette. "My mum says the police will never find them. It's not a serious enough crime for them to bother with. They've got murderers and terrorists to catch."

"I think Lynette's right," Edward said. "If we want to see our bikes again, or at least to stop it happening to other people, we have to do something ourselves." He put his hand in his pocket as he finished speaking.

"Oh, my word, you've done it already, haven't you?" Lynette said, grinning. "You've written a plan."

"Yes I have," Edward said. He unfolded the piece of paper he'd taken out of his pocket.

Caitlin wasn't sure she liked being outvoted, but she was curious about the plan.

Edward came and sat between the girls. On the paper, he'd drawn a map showing the path from the Hermitage gate to the ice house. He'd also marked in the Visitor Centre, the bike racks and the ice house itself. "If we go to the Hermitage at the same time as we did yesterday and hide ourselves in the ice house, we can watch the bike racks without being seen. If the thieves come back, we'll see them and call the police—catch them red-handed."

"But what if nobody comes with a bike. After all there were no other bikes besides ours yesterday. And even if another cyclist does come, there's no guarantee the thieves will come back," Caitlin said.

"Bait," Edward said.

"What?" Caitlin and Lynette said together.

"We use bait," Edward replied. "Like when I go fishing

with my dad. This afternoon, we take a bike with us as bait. My dad says the thieves are probably well organised and will be watching in parks and streets and gardens all during the summer. And if they see their chance, they'll take it. Yeah, okay it might take a few days but I think they'll be back."

"Where are you going to get another bike from?" Lynette asked.

"I'll use my dad's," Edward said.

"And he doesn't mind?" Caitlin asked.

"He doesn't know," Edward said. "He bought it ages ago. He was going to cycle to work on it. But that only lasted about a week. It just sits in the shed now. He'll not even know it's gone. It's a bit big for me, but I can wheel it."

"Good!" Lynette said, jumping up. "We have a plan and we'll keep going back every day until we catch them. So, let's get our lunch and then meet same time as yesterday, at the Hermitage gate, yeah?"

Caitlin still didn't believe they had a chance of catching the bike thieves, but she did think that going on a stakeout was more exciting than sitting at home for the rest of the holidays, and at least she'd be away from Crazy Lady. She stood up. "Okay then. Let's do it."

"Good," Edward said, putting the map back in his pocket.

As soon as she got home, Caitlin went through to the kitchen. This time the kitchen smelled of newly baked bread, another smell Caitlin recognised from her granny's kitchen.

Sure enough there was a loaf cooling on the wire rack. Bella was chopping stuff on a board on the worktop. "Did you have a nice morning?" she asked.

"Yes, thanks," Caitlin said. "Where's Jack Russell?" She looked around for the little dog.

"He's out in the garden. Call him in if you want, he's been outside for a while."

Caitlin saw the dog as soon as she stepped out of the back door. He was lying at the end of the decking, basking in a patch of sunlight. Caitlin also noticed that the bird feeders, which were dotted around the garden and which hadn't been filled up for ages, not since her Mum died, were all full again. Caitlin had a funny feeling, seeing them all full again and lots of birds flitting to and fro, twittering and gathering seed and pecking at the peanuts just like they once had. It was like her mum wasn't really gone, like she could be close by. Caitlin shivered and rubbed her arms. She pushed the thought of her mother away and walked over to the little dog. "Hello, Jack Russell," she said.

Jack sat up and wagged his tail. He raised his paw as Caitlin patted his head.

"Come on," she said. "Time to go inside." He followed her back to the kitchen and went straight to his water bowl for a long drink.

"Lunch is almost ready," Bella said. "Could you set the table and get yourself a drink."

Caitlin went to the cutlery drawer. "What are we having?"

"I'm doing us a nice big salad and we can have some of the bread I just baked."

Caitlin took knives and forks over to the table. She wasn't very keen on salad.

"Don't worry," Bella said. "You'll like this one." She brought a large glass bowl to the table.

She's doing it again, thought Caitlin. She's reading my mind.

"I prefer tomato soup or jam sandwiches for lunch," Caitlin said, pouring herself a glass of milk and thinking how she missed Susie. Susie had always made tomato soup or jam sandwiches for school holiday lunches.

"Yes, I know you do, and I know Susie did her best. But this is better for you and it tastes lots better too."

Caitlin shrugged and sat at the table. Jack curled up at her feet. Bella put a couple of spoonfuls of the salad on Caitlin's plate and then cut her some bread.

"Butter's there if you want it," said Bella, pointing at a blue dish that Caitlin had never seen before. They normally just spread stuff straight from the tub. Caitlin wished things could get back to normal. Susie gone, her bike gone, her mum... Again she pushed away all thoughts of her mum and a little sigh escaped. It was a long time since her mother had died. Caitlin had only been in Primary Five. But she still got a pain in her tummy and her throat when she thought about her.

Bella sat opposite Caitlin and helped herself to salad and bread. Caitlin didn't look up. She just buttered her bread and began eating. She only took a small mouthful of the salad at first, but it was actually really nice. There was tuna, pasta, sweetcorn, tomato, red and green pepper and lettuce, which was cut into little strips, so it was easy to eat, and there was also mayo mixed through it.

Soon she was shovelling big forkfuls of the stuff into her mouth and munching the delicious bread as well. The pain in her tummy and throat disappeared. She looked up to see that Bella was looking at her and she was smiling her twinkly smile.

Caitlin couldn't help smiling back.

"Better?" Bella asked.

"Yes," Caitlin said.

"And you like the salad?"

"Yes—thank you," Caitlin said.

"You must ask Lynette and Edward to join us for lunch or tea one day. I'd like to meet them," Bella said.

Caitlin surprised herself by saying, "Yes, that would be nice." She wondered why she'd said that. The last thing she wanted was her friends meeting Scary Lady in the flesh.

As they ate, the sound of the birds chirping in the garden drifted in through the open kitchen windows. "Was it you who filled up the bird feeders?" Caitlin asked.

"Yes," Bella said. "It seemed such a shame to have them

empty. Birds are our friends, Caitlin. Some even say they carry the souls of those who've gone before us."

Caitlin thought about this for a minute. Then she said, "That's a bit creepy. It's not true is it? They are just birds aren't they?"

Bella shook her head. "No living thing is *just* anything. All life is important. And birds are very special. After all, who knows where they really go when they fly away? I'm not sure about them carrying souls, but I do know they can carry messages."

"Like carrier pigeons? My seanair told me that pigeons carried messages in World War Two. We watched something on TV about it."

"Yes, like that, but not just pigeons and not just in real time," Bella said.

Caitlin frowned, trying to understand.

Bella laughed. "I know it sounds strange. But just remember, Caitlin, look after the birds and they'll look after you."

"Right," Caitlin said, buttering another piece of bread.

When they'd finished eating, Bella unhooked her bag from the back of the chair she was sitting on. She took out the snowstorm ornament and shook it. She tutted and muttered something under her breath before putting it back in the bag. Then she asked Caitlin what her plans for the afternoon were. She seemed pleased, relieved almost, when Caitlin said that she and her friends were going to the Hermitage and that they were going to spend a bit of time watching the bike racks. "If you do see anything suspicious, you go straight to the Visitor Centre and ask them to call the police. You don't go tackling anyone, okay?"

"Okay," Caitlin said.

"I'm so glad you haven't been put off going there by what happened to your bikes. It's such a lovely place, quite magical and mysterious, don't you think?"

"Mmm," Caitlin said, nodding. She hadn't thought of the

Hermitage as magical or mysterious, but when she considered it now, she realised it did feel different to other parks.

"The light is softer," Bella said. "And the sounds are—are different. I suppose it's all those ancient trees and the links with times past."

Again, Caitlin wasn't sure what Bella was on about. She glanced at her watch. "I need to go soon," she said.

Bella unhooked her bag from the back of the chair once again. This time she glanced at the bag's embroidered clock face. "It is indeed later than I thought," she said, replacing it on the back of the chair. She stood up and took the bread that was left over to the bread bin.

Caitlin frowned to herself. It was a clock made from sewing. It surely couldn't tell the time, could it? She looked round at the bag and its clock while Bella's back was turned. She was amazed to see that the hands on the clock were in a different position from the first time she'd seen the bag. They were no longer at five-to-twelve but now showed one minute-to-twelve. But that wasn't the right time. She wondered why Bella hadn't just looked at her watch or the kitchen clock. Then Caitlin noticed a little strip of tartan tied to the bag's strap. She was sure that hadn't been there before and she was also sure it was the same sort of tartan as Edward had taken from the tree to put on his mapstick. She considered asking Bella about it, and about the clock, but decided against it. Instead she took her dishes over to the sink. She wondered if she should offer to help with the washing-up. She guessed Bella would be doing it by hand.

"It's all right," Bella said. "Leave the dishes. I'll do them. You go off and meet your friends. It seems today's the day. Oh, and I made a picnic for you all, it's in the fridge. Oh, and take Jack Russell. Yes, take wee Jack too."

Chapter Seven

"So, you're saying you think Bella can read your mind?" Lynette said.

They were walking along the Hermitage path and Jack, who was now off the lead, trotted along beside them, occasionally dashing off the path and reappearing up ahead. Lynette and Edward had been delighted to meet the little dog and thought it was awesome that Bella had let Caitlin bring him.

Edward, with a pair of binoculars hanging around his neck, walked alongside the girls, pushing his dad's bike. He had his duffle bag over one shoulder and poking out of it was his mapstick.

"I know it sounds silly," Caitlin said. "But she actually guessed I didn't like the sound of what was for lunch, she also knew that I was all right when I was late back, *and* she knew I was missing Susie."

"It's not that strange. Most kids don't like salad, and you weren't that late, and of course you'd be missing Susie," Lynette said. "There's no way Scary Lady has spooky powers. It's just she wants you to think she has."

Caitlin supposed that made sense, but she still felt that Bella could see inside her head. "What about her putting the cake and stuff in my new bag yesterday, even though she couldn't have known I was going to take it with me?"

But before Lynette could answer, Edward asked, "Has she put in any food today?"

"Yes, yes she has. She's made us a picnic. And that's another thing. She'd made the picnic for us before she knew we were coming here, before she knew I was even seeing you two this afternoon."

"She could be guessing, or she could be reading your mind. But it's good that she gives us nice food," Edward said. "What's in the picnic?"

"Never mind that now," Lynette said. "We're nearly at the ice house—and," she pointed towards the Visitor Centre, "it looks like you didn't need to bring your dad's bike after all. There's already three bikes chained to the rack."

"But I did have to bring it," Edward said. "I had to bring it just in case there weren't any others because—"

"Yes, yes, I know," Lynette said. "Give me your duffle bag, and go and chain the bike up. Then we can get settled into our hideout."

The girls watched as Edward padlocked his father's bike beside the others and then walked back up to join them.

As Lynette gave him back his bag, she said, "Let's see the mapstick."

Edward pulled it from the bag and held it up.

"It looks really good, Ed," Lynette said, "now that you've tied on the sketches and the feathers and the pine cone. And you've even drawn the cake! It's a complete record of our walk yesterday with everything in the right order."

"Yes, that's the point of doing it, Edward said. "Although I didn't put on anything that showed that our bikes got stolen. I thought that would spoil it."

"Yeah, quite right," Caitlin said. "It's lovely, so colourful with all the wool. But I wonder where the bit of material came from; how it ended up on the branch."

Edward shrugged, as he returned the stick to his bag. "I looked up the pattern in the book you gave me. It's Royal Stuart tartan. That's the clan tartan of Bonnie Prince Charlie. You know, the guy your locket came from."

"Really?" Caitlin said. "That's a strange..." She remembered the goldfinch with the material in its beak.

"Coincidence?" Edward finished for her. "Caitlin?"

She shook herself. "Coincidence, yes."

"Come on you two," Lynette said. "We better get under cover."

Caitlin let Edward and Lynette go into the ice house ahead of her. They crouched down on the floor, near the doorway, looking out. It took their eyes a few minutes to adjust to the gloom inside the house. According to Edward's watch, it was 2:34. Edward said they should do ten minutes each with the binoculars. He also produced his customary notebook and pen from his bag. He took first watch. Nobody went in or out of the Centre and nobody went near the bike racks. Caitlin and Lynette played a game on Lynette's DS and Jack very obediently lay down when Caitlin told him to.

Then it was Caitlin's turn. She decided to stand just outside the ice house to carry out her observations. As on the day before, she had the weirdest feeling someone was watching her, but when she looked round there was nobody to be seen. After a couple of minutes, two people appeared from the direction of Blackford Hill. It was a man and a woman and they headed towards the bikes. She raised the binoculars to her eyes.

"Two adults going to the bikes," she whispered. The other two jumped up and came to stand behind her. They peered over her shoulder.

"Where?" Lynette and Edward said together.

"Oh, they've—no, I can't see them now," Caitlin said, peering through the binoculars. "That big tree's in the way. They've gone round the side of the bike stand."

"Come on," Edward said. "We need to get a bit closer." He pushed past the girls. They and Jack followed him to the big tree. It really was massive. The three of them stood behind the thickest of its two trunks and peeped through the gap between them. Sure enough there was a man and a woman standing by the bikes.

"They don't look like bike thieves," Lynette said.

"Shh!" Caitlin and Edward said.

"Well, they don't," Lynette whispered. "They look like somebody's mum and dad. Just ordinary and boring."

"They're not going to wear a sign saying *bike thieves* are they?" Edward hissed.

Caitlin looked through the binoculars. "Ah," she said under her breath.

"Ah?" Lynette whispered.

"The man, he's got a key. He's unlocking the padlocks on both the bikes at the far end." Caitlin spoke softly, but she was no longer whispering.

"So, not thieves then," Lynette said. "I told you!"

"Right your turn," Edward said to Lynette, checking his watch. "We should stay here by this old granny pine. There's a better view."

"*Granny* pine?" Caitlin said.

"Yes," Edward said. "That's what such old Scots pine trees are called. He rubbed his hand on the flaking red bark of the main trunk. This one's probably about two hundred years old. But there's even older ones up north."

While Lynette kept watch, Caitlin sat down at the base of the tree with Jack in her lap. She stroked and patted him and rubbed his ears. Edward made more notes in his notebook. Of course Lynette soon got bored with being on lookout duty, and it wasn't long before she was pirouetting and prancing around the tree, with the binoculars swinging about her body.

"Stand still!" Edward said in a sort of subdued splutter.

"I'm bored!" Lynette said.

"You've only been watching for four minutes," Edward whispered.

"This was a daft idea. Nobody's going to come nicking

bikes two days running. They'd have to be pretty daft bicycle nickers." She burst out laughing. "Bicycle nickers, ha, ha, ha. Get it?"

"Keep your voice down!" Edward sighed.

"Let's have our picnic," Caitlin suggested. She didn't want the other two falling out and she agreed with Lynette that they were probably wasting their time. But she didn't want to upset Edward by saying so. He always got so into things, so carried away and doing this was taking his mind off losing both his bike and his American mapstick all in one day.

"Good idea," Lynette said.

"Yep, okay," Edward said. He never could resist food.

"We can sit back against the tree," Caitlin said. "We'll hear if anyone goes past."

They had just started eating the raspberry jam sandwiches when it happened. Jack was still sitting in Caitlin's lap, hoping to catch a crumb or two no doubt. Edward was writing in his notebook while he ate and Lynette leant across to see what he was writing.

"Don't be so nosey!" Edward said.

"I'm not being nosey," Lynette replied, rubbing her arm. "I just wanted..."

Lynette's voice faded into the background. Caitlin was barely aware of her friends anymore. Her attention had been caught by a little bird—a goldfinch¬—that had landed on the grass beside her. It seemed to be staring at her, looking right into her eyes. It cocked its head as she stared back at it, and then it blinked and it seemed as if it was looking into her mind, into her thoughts. Caitlin shivered, felt goosebumps on her arms. A sudden gust of wind ruffled the old pine's branches.

Caitlin heard Edward say something to Lynette and then he pushed her.

Lynette tipped back against the tree trunk and hit it hard with her arm. "Ow!" she cried.

Caitlin felt the ground rumble and shake beneath her. And then the ground seemed to give way and all three of them were falling—falling like Alice down the rabbit hole. Down they went. Caitlin clutching her backpack and Jack, Edward holding his notebook and only just snatching up his duffle bag in time,and Lynette still gripping a sandwich. They screamed in the darkness as down and down they tumbled and twisted. Jack yelped and whined. It was like being on some sort of giant flume. Eventually they saw light ahead. They thudded to a stop on a grassy mound at the base of a large tree. They were in the middle of a big empty field. For a few seconds none of them spoke.

Chapter Eight

"What just happened?" Lynette said.

"I don't know," Caitlin said. "It happened after you hit the tree trunk. It was like a button was pressed and the ground opened up."

"Yes, I got that," Lynette said, "but how, why?"

Caitlin released her grip on Jack and stood up. "And where are we now?" she said as she looked around the field.

"Still in the Hermitage, obviously," Edward said, getting to his feet. He stood beside Caitlin. "There must be a hole under the tree. Maybe its roots have weakened the ground and we slipped down a slope."

"This place doesn't look like the Hermitage," Caitlin said. "And we fell such a long way, we should be underground, not out in the open like this." Jack sniffed the air and let out a little whimper. "It's okay." Caitlin bent down to pat him. "Don't be scared." She reached into her pocket for his lead. "Just till we know where we are," she said as she clipped the lead to his collar.

Lynette got up and walked round the tree before joining the other two. "And where's the end of the tunnel, or chute, or whatever it was?" she said. "We dropped out the end of it, so where's it gone? All that's here's this tree and it's another of your granny pines by the look of it, Ed." She ran her hand down one of the three soft red trunks.

"So it is," Edward said. "An even older one going by the size of it."

There was the rumble of thunder in the distance. Caitlin felt frightened. They had no idea where they were, and no idea how to get back. And she was fairly certain they were no longer even in the Hermitage, although there was something familiar about it. She shiveredonce again, and not just because this place was colder and damper than the sunny afternoon they appeared to have left behind. "So what do we do?" she asked.

"This is scary. None of it makes any sense," Lynette said.

"Everything makes sense," Edward said. "It's just that, sometimes, when we see something for the first time we don't understand it. We need someone to explain the rules. Then we'll know what to do. There's no need to be scared."

"Right, so who do we ask?" Lynette held out her arms and glanced from side to side. "There aren't a lot of people about."

They looked all around them. This place was no field. No crops grew. No animals grazed. There was no fencing. This was moorland and the ground was rough and covered in tussocks of grass. The ground sloped upwards towards the horizon. And now the booming of the thunder was accompanied by intermittent loud cracks and smoke drifted upwards in the distance.

"Edward's right. We just need to find someone to ask," Caitlin said. "I think we should walk up to the top and see if there are houses or something on the other side. That smoke must belong to somebody.

"Come on, then. Let's go," Lynette said and she strode off before the other two could reply.

As they walked, the thunderous noise became louder and the curls of smoke grew thicker. Jack strained at the lead and whined. He pulled back, seeming reluctant to go any further. But Caitlin kept urging him on. By the time they approached the top of the slope, the noise was deafening. The ground shook with each bang and the smoke was all around them, blocking the daylight, stinging their eyes and burning the backs of their throats.

"I don't think that's thunder," Caitlin said. Her eyes watered and she coughed as she spoke. Edward and Lynette were also choking and spluttering.

"So what is—"

A voice, which could only just be heard over the banging, interrupted Lynette's question. But it wasn't just the noise that made it difficult to understand what the voice said. The language didn't seem to be English. Before she could turn to see who'd spoken, Caitlin's arm was grabbed and she was pulled to the ground. She lay face down in a small ditch, Jack at her side. Lynette almost landed on top of her and, as she struggled to turn her head, Caitlin saw Edward stumble to his knees as if he'd been pushed from behind. He too fell down beside her. The banging was deafening. They all covered their ears and closed their eyes. Caitlin clutched Jack very, very tightly.

Eventually the gaps between the bangs got longer. They heard men's voices shouting on the other side of the hill. There were angry shouts, terrible shouts, shouts of pain, and what sounded like shouted commands.

Caitlin raised her head a little and looked up. Crouched in front of them was a boy, his back to the hill. Red hair poked out from under his blue beret, and he seemed not much older than them, fourteen or fifteen maybe. He wore a kilt and a jacket, with a collarless shirt underneath. And on his beret there was a badge of knotted white ribbon. He also had, what looked like, a tartan blanket wound around his back and over one shoulder. Around his nose and mouth, he'd tied a piece of grubby, grey cloth. Tear tracks marked a pink path down his smoke-blackened face. Caitlin moved to a kneeling position. She looked at the boy and raised her eyebrows, checking it was all right to move.

The boy nodded and frowned. He sat facing them. He

moved the cloth down from his mouth and said something. Lynette and Edward sat up too, looking puzzled. But Caitlin recognised the language.

"Gaelic," Caitlin said. "Like my seanair—my granddad— speaks. She took a moment to work out how to say she couldn't really speak Gaelic, then she turned back to the boy. "Chan eil Gaidhlig," she said, shaking her head. "English?"

The boy narrowed his eyes and looked at them suspiciously before replying in English. "I said don't stand up and show yourself above the hill."

"Why not?" Lynette asked.

"Because they'll blow your heads off," the boy said. He looked at Lynette as if he thought she was really stupid.

"Yeah, right," Lynette said, trying, and failing, not to sound scared.

"Who will blow our heads off and why would they want to?" Edward asked. He just sounded curious, not afraid.

"The Redcoats of course," the boy said. "If they see us here, on the side of the Prince's men, they'll point their muskets right at us."

"Redcoats? Prince's men?" Caitlin said.

"Cannons!" Lynette said.

"Is this some kind of battle re-enactment?" Edward asked. "One of my uncles does this sort of thing at the weekends," he said to the girls. "Him and lots of other people pretend to fight old battles from history."

"It's a battle all right," the boy said. "But it's not an old battle and the Young Pretender's not pretending. Prince Charlie's fighting for his life and his kingdom."

"Prince Charlie?" Lynette said. "What, you mean Prince Charles, Prince William's dad, the Queen's son? He's here and he's in a fight? That's—"

"Shh," Edward said, putting his hand on Lynette's arm.

"Don't tell me to shush!" Lynette said.

"No," Edward said. "I mean I think I've worked out where

we are." He stared at the red-haired boy. "You mean Bonnie Prince Charlie, don't you? And this is Culloden." As the boy nodded, Edward turned to the girls and said, "It's 1746 and we're at the battle of Culloden."

Chapter Nine

Caitlin gasped and Lynette giggled. But Caitlin knew Lynette's giggle was more scared than happy. It was like Lynette wanted Edward to be joking but knew he wasn't. Caitlin looked from Edward to the red-haired boy and back to Edward again. She wasn't just amazed at what he'd said; she was also astonished that he seemed so calm about it.

"It's gone very quiet," Edward said.

"I think it's over," the boy replied. "We'll wait some minutes yet and then go and see what's happened. I'm Ewen, by the way. Ewen Cameron."

"Cameron?" Caitlin said. And, as she spoke, she realised she recognised the tartan Ewen was wearing. It was indeed the Cameron one.

"Yes, which clan are you? With your strange clothes and ignorance of Gaelic, you must be Lowlanders," Ewen said.

Lynette, looked Ewen up and down. "Our clothes aren't half as strange as yours. And we're not ignorant. I'm from Edinburgh, if that's what you mean by Lowlander, and I'm proud of it. My name's Lynette Maclean, but I don't belong to any clan."

"As I thought," Ewen said. He leapt to his feet. His hand went to his waist and he reached under the tartan blanket he wore. He pulled out a large dagger and waved it at them. Edward and the girls jumped up and moved back from him.

Lynette grabbed Caitlin's hand and they exchanged frightened glances. With her free hand, Caitlin surreptitiously slid her phone from her pocket and glanced at the screen. No signal. She shoved it back into her pocket.

"Redcoat spies!" Ewen moved towards the three friends.

"We're not spies," Edward said, stepping in front of the girls. "Look." He swung his duffle bag off his shoulder and pointed at the mapstick poking out of the top. "Here, I have Royal Stuart tartan." He pointed at the scrap of material.

Ewen looked at it. "It's not much of a flag, but it's the Prince's tartan, right enough."

"We're not from here. You're right about that," Edward continued. "But we don't want to hurt anybody and we don't want to be hurt. So could you please put that away?" He nodded at the dagger.

Ewen glanced at the girls. He put the dagger back beneath the folds of material. "Hmm, I suppose even King George and his Redcoats aren't desperate enough to send two weakling girls to do their dirty work."

Caitlin felt Lynette's hand tighten its hold on hers, sensed Lynette's outrage at Ewen's remark. Lynette let go of Caitlin's hand and was about to push Edward out of the way to get at Ewen.

But Edward, without even turning round, put out an arm to stop her. He said to Ewen, "I'm Edward by the way. Edward Farquharson and I'm from Edinburgh too."

Ewen just looked Edward up and down before turning to Caitlin. "And you? You been sent from the capital too, a Lowlander like the other two?"

"No, well, that is yes, I live in Edinburgh. I was born there."

"But you know Gaelic?"

"Not really. My mother was from Skye and my seanair and granny, they speak Gaelic."

"And your name?"

Caitlin swallowed. "Caitlin Cameron."

"Cameron!" Ewen frowned and peered at her, touched

his hair as he looked at hers. "I know there are Lowlanders who fought on our side today. They're not all on the side of King George that's for sure. But I thought all Cameron people lived here in the Highlands."

Caitlin shook her head, unsure what to say. Then she remembered her backpack. "My bag," she said and turned so he could see it. "The tartan is the same as yours. It's Cameron."

Ewen glanced at it and nodded. "And your father, he's loyal to my father, here for the fight?"

"Loyal to your father?" Caitlin asked.

"Yes, my father, Cameron of Locheil, your clan chief. He called all Cameron men to fight for Prince Charlie and the Jacobite cause."

"I see," Caitlin said. "Yes, my father, he's loyal."

Ewen nodded, seemingly impressed by this.

Caitlin wasn't at all sure that she did see, and she doubted very much that her father was here. But she sensed they needed to keep Ewen on their side if they were going to figure out what had happened.

"I think we should be getting back," Lynette said.

"Back where?" Ewen asked.

"To Edinburgh, to real life," Lynette said.

"You'll not be setting off today," Ewen said. "The men will want some rest and the Prince will have to decide what he wants to do. What we need to do now is to approach the battle area, make sure the Redcoats have gone —for now at least. Then we must find my father and see where we are to spend the night."

"What are Redcoats?" Lynette asked.

Ewen spat on the ground. Caitlin had never seen such a hate-filled expression on anyone's face. He peered at Lynette as if he couldn't quite believe what he was hearing. "Redcoats are our enemies, of course! They're the reason we fought today."

Lynette looked at Caitlin and Edward. She turned her back on Ewen and whispered to them. "Do you know what he's on about? What's this, this Culloden place, and all this about Lowlanders and Highlanders? And doesn't he know he can get arrested for carrying a knife?"

"I think it was probably okay to carry a knife in 1746," Edward whispered.

"Yeah, yeah whatever," Lynette said. "But this is the twenty-first century and we need to go home. So let's go and find the path and make our way back to the gate and leave Ewen to his war games."

Caitlin glanced at Ewen. He didn't seem to be paying them much attention. He was scrabbling under a bush and pulling something out from under it. "I don't think it's going to be that easy," Caitlin said.

"Why not?" Lynette asked.

"Because," Edward said, "we're more than two hundred and sixty years, and about a hundred and twenty miles from home. It's 1746 and the battle of Culloden has just taken place over there."

"A battle,1746, no way," Lynette said. She looked at Caitlin. "You don't believe him, do you?"

"I don't know," Caitlin said. "I don't think we're in the Hermitage, and just the look and feel of this place, it doesn't feel like summer in Edinburgh. There's no traffic noise, no people—well, no ordinary people. And it does look like Culloden. I think I recognise it. Granny and Seanair brought me here last week. It's near Inverness. There was a battle. Bonnie Prince Charlie, the one I said gave the silver locket to my ancestor Flora Macdonald, he and his army fought against the King's Redcoat soldiers here. Prince Charlie thought he had more of a right to be king than the actual King. If he'd won, he'd probably have been crowned. But King George's Redcoats won. The Prince had to escape to France. He's now a sort of Scottish hero. There's a museum here with stuff all about the battle, but I can't see the car park or the exhibition place."

"Wait a minute," Lynette said. "I know what this is. It's some Edinburgh festival thing. A what do you call it? A fringe show? My gran took me to one last year in the Botanical Gardens. Only she didn't tell me there was going to be a show. And we were walking through the gardens and suddenly this group of people in weird costumes jumped out and danced about and said they were spirits of the garden or something. For the first few minutes I thought it was for real. That's what this is. The Hermitage is having some daft fringe show." She looked over at Ewen who was now standing watching them. He was holding a drum and had a large pack on his back.

"Told you," Lynette said to the other two. "Why would he have a drum, if he wasn't in a show? Hey, Ewen," she called. "What's the name of your show?"

"My show?"

"Yeah, you're in a drama group, aren't you? All that noise we heard, that was the rest of the actors, right? Do we move on now or do they come to us? And when do you play your drum?"

"Actors? Show? Don't you ever talk sense?" Ewen said. "I played my drum whilst the men took up their lines, me and the other drummer boys. My father says it's good for the men. The drumming calms their nerves and stirs their hearts. I just wish he'd let me stay and fight like the other boys. But he said I must keep safe. I must stay alive so the Camerons would have a leader if anything happened. If he didn't—survive."

"He's very good," Lynette said, laughing. "And the year, what year is it?"

"1746," Ewen gave her a funny look. "Girls really are stupid," he said. And before Lynette could answer he added, "Now we better get moving. Keep close to me and be ready to hide if we see any of Cumberland's men."

Edward followed immediately. Caitlin was unsure what to do, what to believe. Lynette took her hand. "Come on," she said. "We might as well see the rest of the show before we go."

The three of them marched briskly behind Ewen, but what they saw when they crested the mound stopped them all in their tracks. Jack barked and growled. Caitlin grasped his lead even more tightly.

Below them was the full expanse of the moor. The boggy brown mud was streaked and puddled with red. And on the blood-soaked ground, on the mounds and in the ditches were bodies. The bodies of hundreds and hundreds of soldiers. And the smell was terrible. The stench of manure, blood and fear made Caitlin feel very sick. Glancing at her friends' pale faces, she knew they felt the same. Caitlin picked Jack up, took off his lead and tucked him under one arm. She didn't think he'd want to have his paws in all the filth. She could feel the little dog's body trembling against her own.

The awful smell of death hung in the air all around them. Somewhere a crow cawed.

A sudden quick movement caught Caitlin's eye. A rat had run out from under a bush and was quickly followed by several more. They scrambled over and around the bodies. Lynette and Edward saw them too. Caitlin took a step back.

Lynette gasped and covered her mouth with her hands. Jack growled and wriggled in Caitlin's arms, all signs of fear gone. He jumped free and ran off to chase the rats. The rats scattered back into the undergrowth when they saw the little dog approaching.

"Did you see them?" Lynette asked, clutching at Caitlin's arm. "Did you see those —those things?" Her terror was etched on her face.

"You'll always get rats where there's dirt and death," Edward said. His voice was its usual matter-of-fact tone, but even he looked quite shocked. "But Jack seems to be able to handle them. I think he'll keep them away from us."

Ewen had kept on walking, unperturbed by the sight of the rats. Suddenly he called, "I must find my father!" He flung down his drum and his pack and ran towards the battlefield.

Edward picked up Ewen's stuff and went after him. The girls moved more slowly, grasping each other's hands. Jack scampered along beside them, his ears pricked up and his body alert. Caitlin and Lynette picked their way past and around the dead and dying men. Their jeans and trainers were soon covered in the disgusting mud.

"This really isn't a show, is it?" Lynette said, shivering.

"No, it isn't a show," Caitlin said. "It was a real battle. All these poor people."

The girls looked around. Most of the soldiers lay very still. But some moaned or cried out in pain. Occasionally one would stretch a hand out towards the girls.

"What should we do?" Lynette said.

"What can we do? They need doctors, the ones who're still alive that is."

They walked on a bit further and made for the edge of the moor. Ewen and Edward were a good distance ahead and were keeping close to the scrubby bushes that ran along the side of the field. The girls had decided to do the same as the bushes would give them a hiding place if they needed one.

When they reached the moor's edge, the girls walked in silence, in single file now, Caitlin following Lynette and keeping Jack to heel beside her. Caitlin heard the groan first and then felt something touch her ankle. She stumbled and let out a yell, terrified it might be rat.

Lynette whirled round. "What is it?" she said. Jack ran around in circles, yelping.

Caitlin looked down. A hand grasped her by the ankle and, lying at her feet, half-hidden by a gorse bush, was a man. His head was bleeding heavily and there was blood seeping through his shirt from his chest. He was dressed just like Ewen in a kilt and blanket thing. Beside him lay his dagger and shield, discarded and useless. Jack barked and growled at the wounded soldier. Caitlin told the dog to be quiet and to sit. She bent down to look at the man. He freed her ankle and grabbed her hand. "Help me!" he said.

When Caitlin looked at his face, she saw that he was probably around the same age as her brother, James, about seventeen or eighteen. His eyes were wide with pain and fear. His skin was pale and Caitlin could see beads of sweat on his forehead.

She tried to pull her hand away but his grip was strong in spite of his injuries.

"We'll get help for you," Caitlin said, trying again to pull her hand away.

But he gripped her even tighter. "Don't leave me!" he said. "Do something, please."

"Okay," Caitlin said. "But you'll have to let go of my hand, so I can try to help you."

He nodded and released his grip, letting out another groan.

Caitlin took off her backpack.

Lynette hopped from one foot to the other. "Don't be long," she said. "Edward and Ewen are almost out of sight. We don't want to lose them. And what if more soldiers come?"

"I'll be as quick as I can," said Caitlin. "You keep an eye on the boys and keep a look out for Redcoats too. This guy's from the Prince's side."

Caitlin knelt down beside the soldier. She tried to remember what she'd learned at Guides about first aid.

"ABC, Airway, Breathing, Circulation," she said. She knew you had to check an injured person wasn't unconscious, and if they were, you checked their tongue wasn't choking them, and then you put them in the recovery position. Then you checked they were breathing and that their heart was beating. But it was obvious that he was breathing and his heart was beating. 'What else?' she thought.

"Bleeding!" she said out loud. "Yes, bleeding. Press on any wounds and stop the flow of blood." She grabbed a handful of tissues from the packet in the front pocket of her backpack and pressed them to the wound on the soldier's head. He winced with the pain. "Sorry," she said. "Can you hold these in place for me?"

He managed to nod and raised his hand to hold onto the tissues.

"Edward and Ewen have stopped walking, " Lynette said. "I think they're talking to somebody. It's difficult to see. Trust Edward to go off with the binoculars!"

"Well they are his. Let me know when they start moving again," Caitlin said. She had another quick, but pointless, look at her phone before turning back to the young man. "What's your name?" she asked.

"Angus Chisholm, from Kincraig," he replied, gritting his teeth as he spoke.

"I'm Caitlin Cameron from Edinburgh, pleased to meet you. We're both a long way from home." As she said this, Bella popped into her head and Caitlin wondered if perhaps… She looked in her backpack. Yes! Bella had done it again, put stuff in the bag that was going to prove very welcome. Besides the remains of the picnic, there, tucked away at the bottom, was a packet of wet-wipes, a small first-aid kit and a towel. Caitlin didn't stop to think how Bella knew these would be needed. She just grabbed them.

After she'd cleaned Angus's head wound with some of the wipes, she took a dressing from the first-aid kit and stuck it over the deep cut. Then she took a deep breath. Angus was shivering and the patch of blood on his shirt was getting bigger. She rolled up the towel and pulled up his coarse, grey shirt. The blood was coming from a wound in Angus's side. Caitlin pressed the towel down on it. Angus winced and groaned.

"Sorry," she said. "It's a really bad cut. I'm trying to get it to stop bleeding."

"It was a bayonet, a damn Redcoat, with a bayonet. I didn't see him coming." He was shivering even more now.

"Press down on this," Caitlin said, placing his hand on the towel. Then she carefully unwound the blanket from his shoulder and used it to cover him.

"The boys are on the move again," Lynette said. "We better go."

"I have to leave you now," Caitlin said to Angus. But I promise I'll try to find someone who can help you."

Angus grabbed her hand and squeezed it. "Thank you," he whispered, his voice now very weak. "You remind me of my mother," he added.

Caitlin had tears in her eyes, as she stood up. "And you remind me of my brother," she said. And with her tears now running down her cheeks, she put Jack on the lead and followed Lynette without looking back.

Chapter Ten

As the girls began to catch up to Edward and Ewen, Edward turned to look for them. He was no longer carrying Ewen's stuff. He raised his free arm and gestured. He seemed to want them to hurry up. They ran the rest of the way. It wasn't until they were almost beside the boys that Caitlin and Lynette saw that there were others, a group of men, standing in a huddle just beyond Edward and Ewen. Judging by their weapons, filthy tartan clothing and black-streaked faces, these men had to be a group of Jacobite soldiers.

"Where did you two get to?" Edward asked, when the girls at last caught up. "I thought you were right behind us, but when I turned round you weren't there."

"We found somebody," Caitlin said, puffing and panting, "A soldier who was injured. I tried to help him, but he needs a proper doctor."

"There are already stretcher bearers checking the battle-field," Ewen said. "If the soldier you found is lucky, they will find him and his wounds will be attended to. Then he'll be taken to shelter."

"I promised him I'd—"

But Caitlin's words were cut off by a shout from one of the men up ahead. "Come on, we must hurry."

"I haven't got my breath back yet!" Lynette said. "Who are they anyway?"

"A band of loyal soldiers. Their leader is the one who shouted. He is Murdo Cameron a cousin of my father,"

Ewen said. "My father is wounded, shot in the legs. Murdo is taking me to him. I've told him who you are. He's not very happy having to look after Lowlanders, especially wee lassies, but—"

"Oh, isn't he?" Lynette said, frowning.

Ewen ignored Lynette's protest. "But I persuaded him. I explained that you'd got separated from your regiments and need to find your clansmen for the journey home. And now the first thing we must do is get off the moor and find some cover. The Redcoats aren't far behind us and Murdo says their orders are to kill any Jacobites they find."

Caitlin wasn't at all sure that they should be following Murdo and Ewen, and she didn't want to let Angus down. She couldn't get his face out of her mind. She hung back. Lynette stopped to wait for her.

Edward looked round at both of them. "Don't get left behind again. Hurry up."

Caitlin beckoned to him. He came to join the girls and Caitlin made sure that the three of them walked together and far enough behind Ewen and Murdo so that they wouldn't be overheard.

"What's wrong?" Edward asked.

"I'm worried about all of this," Caitlin said. "I want to get help for Angus, but even more than that I want to get home. I'm not sure that following these men is what we should be doing."

Lynette nodded. "I'm with you there. I think we should head for home."

Now it was Edward who halted. "And how will we do that?" he said.

The girls stopped and turned to him.

"I don't know," Caitlin said. "I've no idea what's going on or how we got here, but I do know I don't want to stay."

"Me neither," Lynette said. "I just want to go home."

"I agree," Edward said. "But I think we're going to need

help to get back, and I think we need an adult to help us. So, for now, I vote we stick with Ewen and go to see his father. He sounds like an important man. He might know what to do."

"But he's injured. He's been shot. Even if we could get to see him, he'll have other things on his mind, like staying alive and getting better," Lynette said.

"Yes, I know, but even if he can't help us, he'll most likely know someone who can. Anyway we better keep moving. We're safer staying with Ewen for now. We don't want to be caught by Redcoats, do we?" Edward started walking again.

The girls followed, walking either side of him. "Ed's right," Caitlin said. "With my phone not working, Ewen's people are probably the only ones who can help us."

"Okay," Lynette said. But she didn't sound convinced.

"Are you three coming with us or not?" Murdo's voice made the three friends jump. They hadn't noticed him making his way back to join them. He stood in front of Caitlin. She noticed the large dagger he had secured in his belt, and over one shoulder there hung a dented shield. "If you want to come with us, you'll need to keep up," he said. "Me and the men haven't got time to wait for three weak Lowlanders."

"Yes," Caitlin said. "We're coming." She looked at Murdo's face. His expression was stern but he also looked very tired, like her dad sometimes did. The smears of soot on his face were streaked pink where sweat—or could it have been tears—had run down. "Sorry," she said. "We *will* keep up. Thanks for allowing us to go with you. We may be Lowlanders, and Lynette and me, yes, we are lassies, but I promise you, we're not weak and we'll not slow you down. We'd really appreciate it if you could take us to Ewen's father."

Murdo's cross expression changed to something that was almost a smile. "Good." He held out a hand. "Murdo Cameron," he said.

Caitlin shook his hand. "Caitlin Cameron and this is Lynette Maclean."

Murdo nodded at Lynette. Then he turned back to Caitlin. "I don't understand why you and Miss Maclean are here today. We have no need of young ladies on the battlefield, but I do know Lowlanders have some strange ideas. And you are a Cameron, so that's good enough for me. We are heading for the Jacobite barracks at Kingussie, some way from here. It's there we hope to find young Ewen's father. You and your friends are welcome to come with us and to our protection, but you must stay close and you must keep up. Understood?"

"Understood," Caitlin said. And Edward and Lynette both nodded at Murdo.

"Good," Murdo said. "And the terrier, I assume he's a good hunter and rat catcher, and that could be useful. But you must keep him under your control at all times, otherwise..."

"Understood," Caitlin said again.

Murdo nodded and then turned and strode off to rejoin the men up ahead.

The three friends walked on in silence, following in the footsteps of Ewen and Murdo and the other men.

It was hard going as the ground was very boggy. The muscles in their legs ached from the effort and progress was slow. And as they walked, more and more crows circled and cawed overhead.

Murdo kept checking that they weren't being followed. Every now and again they heard musket fire in the distance. Eventually they left the moor behind and arrived at a rough road.

"My legs are sore," Lynette said. "And I'm starving. It must be dinnertime at home."

Caitlin glanced at her watch, but like her mobile phone it seemed to have stopped working.

Edward pointed at his own watch. "Mine's not working either," he said.

"Maybe we'll stop soon for a rest and then we can eat what's left of the picnic," Caitlin said.

"Do you think we should ask for a break?" Lynette said "And I could do with finding a toilet soon too."

"I don't think Murdo will want to stop just yet," Edward said. "As for the toilet, you'll have to find a bush to go behind. That's what I did."

"I don't think so!" Lynette gasped. "I'll wait till we come to a proper loo."

Before Edward or Caitlin could explain that plumbed-in, flushing toilets were unlikely to appear anywhere soon, Murdo glanced back at the three children and raised an arm. He pointed at the roadside. "We must get off the road," he called. "We'll cross the ditch and drop down behind the trees. We can still keep to the route, but remain hidden if the Duke's men come riding along."

The ditch was full of fast flowing water and it was quite a leap and a scramble to get over it. The ground sloped away on the other side and they walked along parallel to, but below the road. Caitlin could see that Murdo was right. The gorse bushes and stumpy trees that grew all along the verge meant they couldn't be seen from the road.

They hadn't gone far when they heard a noise that sounded like distant drumming.

"This is it," Murdo said. "Get down and stay hidden till my signal."

They all crouched low behind the bushes. The noise was louder now and unmistakable. The drumming was actually the beat of hooves on the hard ground. Caitlin heard the snorting breaths of the horses as they grew nearer. She peered upwards through the jagged gorse branches. All she could see were the horses' galloping legs along with flashes of red, and glimpses of boots in stirrups. Then one set of galloping legs came to a halt directly above her. The following set of legs also stopped and the riders of both horses dismounted.

Caitlin's mouth suddenly felt very dry. Petrified, she kept her head down and her eyes closed. She was scared even to breathe. She put a hand around Jack's muzzle to stop him barking and held him close, but the dog seemed to sense the need for quiet and didn't make a sound.

"What's wrong?" said a voice. The voice of one of the riders.

"He's gone lame. Stone in the shoe I reckon," said the other, younger-sounding voice.

"Get it out and be quick about it. We shouldn't get separated from the others. We could be set upon by Jacobites at any moment."

"I doubt there's many of them left. We got most of them on the field and we've dispatched a fair few in the chase. The Major said we'd only be checking out one more of their villages and then we'd be turning back to Inverness."

Gradually, Caitlin's curiosity overcame her fear. Despite her pounding heart, she couldn't resist moving from her crouching position to a kneeling one in order to get a better look. She could see both Redcoats. The younger of the two was bent over one of his horse's back hooves. The other soldier was holding onto his horse's reins and looking around nervously.

"I don't see any stone," said the stricken horse's rider. "Come on, boy," he said, pulling the reins. But the horse just whinnied and refused to move.

Caitlin glanced along at Edward to see if he was watching. But Edward was crouched behind Ewen's pack and had his head down and his hands over his ears. Then she looked at Lynette and gasped at what she saw.

Lynette had somehow got hold of Edward's binoculars and was now standing, watching the soldiers through them. She was only partly hidden behind a tree.

But before Caitlin could signal to Lynette to get down, the older soldier spoke. "He always was a strange one," he said. "Always seemed he was in charge of you, instead of the other way around. If he's decided he's not going any further then there's probably no point in even trying to force him."

"So, what do I do?" the first soldier said.

His comrade shook his head and got up on his horse. "Well, you can either stay here with him and wait for the Prince's men to come and cut your throat, or you can leave him here to his fate, and come along with me."

"I can't leave him, I've had him since he was a foal. We've been in many battles together and I owe him my life. He's the bravest horse I've ever known. Worthy of his name, aren't you, Hero?"

The horse tossed his head and then nuzzled the soldier's neck and shoulder. The soldier put his arms around the horse's neck and seemed to be whispering in the horse's ear. The horse snorted and whinnied.

"He's not going any further, not with me at any rate. It seems he has his reasons."

"Reasons? He's a horse, just a stubborn old horse. Are you coming or not? If we don't get going we could end up permanently separated from the others."

"Yes, yes I'm coming," replied the first soldier. He patted the horse's nose. "Goodbye, old friend and farewell." The horse pawed the ground and bowed its head. The soldier turned away. He grabbed his comrade's outstretched arm and swung himself up onto the saddle. He didn't look back as they galloped off.

For a few moments after the two Redcoats had gone, nobody moved. Caitlin noticed that Lynette had ducked back down, but she still had the binoculars around her neck. It was Murdo who stood up first. He signalled to the others to come out of their hiding places.

Caitlin nudged Edward, who at last looked up. "It's all right, Ed. They're gone. The soldiers are gone."

Murdo beckoned for them all to gather round and said,

"It seems, from what the Redcoat said that that was probably the last of them for now."

"Good," Lynette said. "So we can stop now, get something to eat, have a rest."

Murdo shook his head. "Not yet. Another hour, then we'll stop, but just for a time. We've as far to go again before dark, then we'll camp till dawn."

"But I'm exhausted," Lynette said.

Murdo looked at her. "Soft Lowlanders," he said. "We've only been walking for a few hours."

Ewen laughed. Lynette glowered at him.

Murdo shook his head and , still looking at Lynette, said, "What's that?" He pointed at the binoculars Lynette was still wearing. "Is that some kind of fancy Lowland scope?"

Lynette put her hand to the strap. She glanced at Edward, a guilty look on her face. But he didn't seem bothered. "They're binoculars," she said.

Lynette raised them to her eyes. "You look through them like this. They make things that are far away look as if they're much closer." She removed the strap from around her neck and handed them to Murdo.

Murdo put the binoculars up to his eyes. He jumped a little as he took in what he could see through them. "My word! It's—that's— oh my word—that horse looks as if it's standing right here. These are better than any telescope I've ever seen."

He lowered them for a moment and Ewen grabbed them. "Let me see!" he cried. The rest of the men, who had paid them little attention until now, gathered round to see what the fuss was about.

Mention of the horse gave Caitlin an idea. She told Jack to stay. Then, while Murdo, Ewen and the men squabbled over the binoculars and asked Lynette how they worked and where she'd got them, she grabbed Edward's hand. "Come with me." She scrambled up the slope towards the road and

Edward followed her.

Hero still stood where his Redcoat rider had left him.

Caitlin approached him. He was big, taller than Sanna, the horse she rode at the riding club, and his coat was shiny black.

"Hallo, boy," she said. She stretched a hand towards the animal. "Hallo, Hero. I'm Caitlin." The horse dropped his head and let out a soft whinny. Caitlin took hold of the reins in one hand and patted the horse's neck with the other. "And this is Edward," she said, glancing over her shoulder. "Come and say hallo, Ed."

Edward, approached the horse. He patted the animal's nose. Hero seemed to lean into Edward and brushed the side of his face. Caitlin stepped to the side, still holding the reins, as Edward put both arms around Hero's neck. They stood like that for a few moments.

When Edward released his hold on Hero, he turned to Caitlin and said, "Hero's here to help us. He knows we're a long way from home and he doesn't want us to be afraid."

Caitlin wasn't sure she believed that Hero had communicated with Edward, but she thought that whatever the horse understood, it would be helpful to take him along with them on their journey. But first, of course, they'd have to see if he could walk. She gave the reins a gentle tug and clicked her tongue. He walked behind her without any difficulty. She led him round in a circle and then back to where Edward was standing.

"Did you see him arriving with the Redcoat soldiers?" she asked Edward.

"Yes, but then I didn't look anymore after that. I didn't want to look at the soldiers."

"His rider thought he had a stone in his shoe. But he obviously hasn't. He just wouldn't move. So his rider left him behind and rode off with another soldier."

"I think Hero knew we were hiding here," Edward said.

Caitlin patted the horse. "I don't know about that, but he seems fine now. We could take him with us. He might not survive out here all alone. We could try to get food for him and we could maybe ride him."

"Maybe," Edward said.

Caitlin led Hero off the road and they walked back to the others. The men were all still busy trying out the binoculars.

Lynette was sitting on a boulder, looking very fed up. She jumped to her feet when she saw them coming. "What are you doing with the horse?" she asked.

"I was wondering the same," Murdo said.

"I thought we could take him with us, " Caitlin said.

"He's a Redcoat horse and a useless one at that," Murdo grunted. "We'll not be wasting any good Highland grass on him."

"He's not useless! And he's not a Redcoat horse, he's just a horse." Edward stood very straight, his hands curled into fists at his side. He looked Murdo in the eye as he spoke. Caitlin and Lynette looked at each other in surprise. They'd seen Edward angry before, but he rarely looked people in the eye, especially strangers. And he even more rarely stood up to anyone. "He's *meant* to be with us. He *will* help us get home."

With that he scooped up Ewen's drum and pack. "Here," he said handing the pack to Ewen. "I'll carry the drum for you." He hitched the drum over one shoulder, checked that his duffle bag—which still had the mapstick sticking out the top—was secure on the other, and grabbed hold of Hero's reins. "We should get moving," he said and set off along the track with the horse walking happily beside him. Murdo stared after him, open-mouthed, and then he threw back his head and laughed. "You heard him. Let's go!"

Chapter Eleven

After about an hour of walking, they arrived at the foot of a hill which had a burn flowing down it.

"We'll take a rest here and have some food," Murdo said. "Then we'll go over the hill and avoid the village those Redcoats were making for." He looked at Caitlin and her friends. "I suppose we'll need to feed you three as well."

"No thank you," Caitlin said. "We've got our own food."

Murdo shrugged. He, Ewen and the men took bread and cheese and stone jars from their packs. They filled their jars with water from the burn.

Following Caitlin's example, Lynette had had to give in and find a bush to hide behind in order to go to the toilet. She made a bit of a fuss about it to say the least, but Caitlin hoped that now Lynette had done it once she wouldn't make such a big deal of it the next time.

Caitlin, Lynette and Edward sat on the grass a little bit apart from the men. Jack sniffed at the grass and ran off before Caitlin could tell him to stay. But something told her he wouldn't go far and she really had enough to cope with right at that moment without looking after him too. She unpacked the picnic that Bella had prepared for them. They were almost too tired to eat. But they did feel better after they'd munched their way through the remaining sandwiches and big slabs of sponge cake, all washed down with apple juice. Bella had even packed some dog biscuits and a slice of chicken for Jack.

While everyone was eating, Hero drank some water from the burn and nibbled at the grass. Caitlin watched him as she ate. He truly was a beautiful animal and she already felt like she knew him as well as Sanna. Sanna was the horse she rode at the riding club and although she loved the little white mare, it had taken Caitlin a while to understand the horse's moods and anticipate what she wanted to do. But Hero was easy to read. He looked so calm and friendly, and she already felt she could trust him completely. She couldn't understand how the Redcoat just abandoned him. She also didn't understand why Hero had pretended to be lame.

Just then Jack reappeared. He wasn't alone. He had a dead rabbit in his jaws, a half-eaten dead rabbit. He dropped it at the children's feet and then got on with eating what was left of it.

Lynette recoiled and was about to scream but Edward put his hand over her mouth. She pushed him away. "What is that? What has he got?"

"He's caught a rabbit," Edward said. "He just did what's natural for him. He hunted and got his dinner."

"Gross!" Lynette said. She moved back slightly from the other two.

Caitlin waved one of the dog biscuits at Jack. He gave it a quick glance but continued with the rabbit. It was when she was putting the biscuits back in her bag that Caitlin noticed the folded piece of paper, stuck in the corner at the bottom. Edward was over by Hero, patting and talking to him and Lynette had regained enough energy and equilibrium to practise her ballet arms. The piece of paper had Caitlin's name written on it. She took it out and unfolded it. It was a note, a note from Bella. It said—

Dear Caitlin,

When you read this you'll probably feel like you've been away from home for ages. You mustn't worry. You are where and when you're meant to be. All is as it should be at home and you won't be missed. I'm watching over you, but it is for you to fulfil your quest. Your friends old and new can help you, including the wonderful Hero. He too is where and when he is meant to be.

Take care and be brave,

Bella

"What's that?" Lynette asked. "You've got a very strange look on your face."

"She knew," Caitlin replied. "Bella knew it all. She knew what was going to happen to us. She says we've not to worry and I've got my friends to help me."

"What do you mean?" Lynette asked.

Caitlin handed her the note.

"Okay, so that's weird and creepy," Lynette said, giving the note back to Caitlin. "Scary Lady really is scary. How does she know we're far away and how the heck does she know about Hero?"

"I've no idea," Caitlin said. "It is certainly weird, but it doesn't make me feel scared. I don't know why, but I think it makes me feel better."

"Hmm," Lynette said in a way that suggested she didn't feel as reassured as Caitlin did. "Should we tell Ed?" she asked. "It could upset him."

Before Caitlin could answer, Edward came over to the girls. "Hero's told me not to worry. He says he's meant to be here now and so are we. We're here for a reason and he will look after us."

"Hero told you?" Caitlin said. She tried to keep her disbelief out of her voice.

Lynette wasn't so gentle. "What? Like he spoke to you?" She laughed. "Ed, he's a horse. He can't tell you anything."

"Of course he didn't speak!" Edward said. "I know he's a horse. But he does communicate with me. I know what he's thinking and that's what he told me. We're supposed to be here."

Caitlin remembered what her father had told her when he'd suggested to Edward's mother that horse-riding might be good for Edward. He'd said that people who have difficulties talking to other people often find that they can get along very easily with horses. He also said that horses seem to be able to understand a lot of stuff without words.

Caitlin certainly agreed with that. After she and Sanna had got to know each other, it was obvious Sanna understood her, knew when she was sad, knew when she was missing her mum. And somehow Sanna could always make Caitlin feel better.

So she wasn't as surprised as Lynette by what Edward had said. However, she did wonder how the horse could have been as precise in what it told Edward.

But, she didn't get very long to think about it because Murdo called over to them that it was time to get going again.

Edward led Hero over to the girls. "You could both ride on him for a while," he said. "Then Lynette won't get so tired."

"I'm fine!" Lynette said. "I don't want to ride a silly old horse."

"He's not silly," Edward said. "And you did say you were tired earlier."

Caitlin knew that Lynette was a bit scared of horses so she said, "You can sit behind me and just hold on tight. I know *I'm* tired. I've never walked so far in my life and Murdo said we had another couple of hours to go before we stop for the night. We'll ride for a while and then Edward can get a shot."

"Come on!" Murdo called.

"We're coming," Caitlin called back.

Lynette frowned, trying to make up her mind. Caitlin asked Edward to give her a boost so she could get onto Hero's back. "I've already shortened the stirrups," Edward said, as Caitlin got settled. "You ready?" he said to Lynette, and he positioned his hands for her to step up.

"Oh, all right," Lynette said.

They set off up the hill. Lynette had her arms around Caitlin's waist and clung on tightly. Edward walked beside them with Jack at his side. They followed Murdo, Ewen and the men up and over the top and down the other side.

Caitlin found Hero very easy to ride even although he was so much bigger than Sanna. She knew her father would have a fit if he saw her riding without her riding hat, and it wasn't something she'd ever do at home, but here, wherever here was, the normal rules didn't seem to apply.

Once they were on the other side of the hill they walked on over another seemingly endless moor. The dull day had changed to deep twilight when Ewen came to walk beside Edward. The boys chatted as they walked. Caitlin couldn't hear everything they said but she caught bits and pieces. Ewen was talking about his home and about his father.

After about an hour, Caitlin offered to get down and let Edward ride for a while. But Edward said that he was all right walking.

At last the moor ended and they came to a rough track. It was almost completely dark when they arrived at the edge of a village. Ewen told them it was called Clachmile. "This is a safe place to stop. The Redcoats will have turned back for Inverness by now and it's a Jacobite village," he said.

Caitlin and Lynette dismounted and Caitlin led Hero along the street, walking behind the others. The only light was the light of the moon, but it was enough to let Caitlin see their surroundings. There were a few small houses huddled close to the dirt-track street. She saw the occasional flicker of candlelight at a few of the tiny windows. About halfway along there was a bigger building. It seemed to be all closed up, but Murdo stopped and knocked on the door. Nobody answered.

"It's not surprising the inn's closed," Murdo said. "Nobody will want to be out and about tonight. But I was hoping to get us somewhere to sleep and a stable for that useless nag. But I have another plan. I've heard the Laird is a reasonable man, a Fraser and sympathetic to the Prince's cause. I know his Tacksman, John Fraser, he lives at Clachmile House. We'll try there. There may well be an outhouse we can use. It's not much further." He looked at Lynette as he made his last remark and despite the low level of light, Caitlin thought she saw a bit of a smile cross Murdo's normally, rather solemn face. "It's just out of the village and up a bit of a hill on the eastern side.

"How do you know, about the inn, and the big house?" Ewen asked Murdo.

"I wasn't always your father's servant," Murdo replied. "When I was your age, me and my brothers and my father would drive my family's cattle through here to the market in Inverness."

"Drive?" Lynette said "But how? How could you drive?"

"How do you think?" Murdo said. "My word, you Lowlanders really don't know much, do you? We walked them, drove them along with the help of a strong stick, over hills and across rivers. We've been following the drove road for the last while."

"Right, I see," Lynette said.

"Good. Now, let's get going," Murdo said.

It wasn't long before Murdo turned in at a pair of wide gates and they all followed him up a broad, gravel driveway. The house at the top of the driveway was huge, its front door solid and wooden. The house itself appeared to be in darkness and the windows were shuttered.

Murdo rapped on the door. There was no reply and so Murdo knocked again. "John Fraser! It's Murdo Cameron, kinsman to Locheil. I seek shelter," he called and banged on the door once more.

At last they heard the sound of the lock turning and of bolts being drawn back. The door opened a crack and a shaft of light shone out. "Murdo, Murdo Cameron, is that you?" said a voice from behind the door.

"Yes, John, it's me. Please, open up and let us in," Murdo said.

The door opened wider and a man appeared. He was dressed like Murdo and Ewen and the other men although he wasn't nearly so disheveled. He looked quite old. Caitlin guessed he must be the same sort of age as her grandfather. He held a glass lantern up beside his head and he looked Caitlin, Lynette and Edward up and down before turning to Murdo. "So, Murdo Cameron, you survived this terrible day and I'm not sorry that you have. What do you want of me?"

"My men and I, we need shelter for the night and a stable for the horse. We are making for the barracks at Kingussie. I have young Ewen, Locheil's son with me. His father was grievously wounded in the battle and was carried away. I must bring his boy safe home."

John Fraser swung the lantern in order to inspect Ewen. "Uh huh," he said. "And these?" He turned the lantern light on Caitlin and her friends.

"Young Lowlanders, drummers and attendants, I believe, got separated from their regiments. The red-haired one is a Cameron and the other girl a Maclean. The young lad is one of Farquharson's people. They seek Locheil's help to get home."

"Uh huh," Fraser said again. "Those Lowlanders are queer folk right enough, sending lassies to the field." He shook his head. "Well, you better come in." He stood back for them to enter.

Caitlin hung back as the others crossed the threshold. She was unsure what to do about Hero. John Fraser looked at her. "Tie your horse at that tree over yonder," he said. "And I'll get one of my men to take him round to the stables at the back. He'll be given a bag of oats and a clean, dry stall. Your terrier will be taken to the stables too, plenty rats there to keep him busy."

Caitlin turned to where Mr Fraser had pointed. In the moon's light, she saw a small tree at the edge of a square of grass in front of the house. "Thank you," she said. For some reason she felt really pleased that Mr Fraser thought that Hero was hers.

Once she had tied his reins round the tree's trunk, Caitlin patted Hero's neck and nose. She whispered goodnight to him and told him she'd see him in the morning. He whinnied softly back. She hugged Jack Russell and told him to stay with Hero. Then Caitlin scurried back over to the house. The door had been left slightly open and she went in, closing it behind her. She found herself in a large, square hall with a broad staircase at the middle of the opposite wall. A coal fire blazed in a huge fireplace at one end, and the hall was lit by flaming torches and candles. The others were all standing near the chairs at the fireside. A woman in a long dress, apron and white frilly cap seemed to be organising everyone.

Mr Fraser saw Caitlin approaching. "And this is one of Murdo's kinsfolk, a Cameron, from Edinburgh. This is Mrs Crawford, my housekeeper."

The woman smiled at Caitlin. She had a kind face. "How do you do, young miss. What's your Christian name?"

"Caitlin, I'm Caitlin Cameron."

"You are all welcome here," Mr Fraser said. "I'm only sorry I'm too old to have been on the field myself this day. I've no doubt you all saw terrible things and that you want to get home. I count myself very fortunate that my own son was spared. I know there are many Frasers who'll not be returning to their homes tonight or ever." He stopped for a moment and looked very sad.

Caitlin thought of Angus and wondered where he was now and if he would be going home soon.

"We already have several wounded men being cared for here, as well as some unharmed, like yourselves, who simply seek shelter. They arrived not long before you but they have already eaten and are bedded down in the dining room and the drawing room. But we'll make room for you all," Mr Fraser said.

"Yes, as I was saying," Mrs Crawford said, "The men and young Master Cameron can have the two bedchambers that are unoccupied upstairs and the other young people can sleep here in the hall. There will be warmth from the fire and I'll make sure they have plenty blankets."

"Good," Mr Fraser said. "Please, everyone, take a seat near the fire and I'll go and see our Mrs Baxter about getting some food for you all."

Caitlin and her friends found it hard to stay awake as they waited for their supper. But they revived a bit after a meal of soup followed by some sort of stew. They ate at a long wooden table in the kitchen. Caitlin thought that the meat in the stew might be rabbit, or maybe deer, but thought it best not to ask in front of Lynette who was tucking in enthusiastically. After they'd eaten, Mrs Crawford came to show Ewen, Murdo and the men where they would be sleeping.

"And you, young ones," she said, "go back to the hall and you'll find what you need for a comfortable night."

It wasn't long before Caitlin, Lynette and Edward were snuggled down side by side on the fireside rug. Mrs Crawford showed them where the privy was and had given them a chamber pot for the night. She'd been very amused when she'd had to explain both the workings of the privy and the purpose of the pot to them.

"Lowlanders!" she'd laughed. "You are funny folk."

After doing their best to brush the now dried mud from their jeans, Caitlin and her friends removed only their sweaters, socks and shoes before lying down on mattresses that seemed to be made of rough cotton stuffed with straw. They were covered by thick, rather scratchy, blankets. But they were so tired, it felt like they were in the comfiest beds in the world.

They talked a little about all that had happened to them that day. Caitlin told Edward about Bella's note. He wasn't all that bothered about its existence, but like the girls he did wonder about its meaning. However, they were all so exhausted that none of them could wonder for very long. And it was only a short time before they all fell asleep.

Chapter Twelve

Next morning, Caitlin awoke as soon as the sunlight fell across her face. Mrs Crawford was at one of the windows and had just opened the shutters. She turned and saw that Caitlin was awake.

"Time to get up," Mrs Crawford said, smiling at her. "Our first group of soldiers are up and breakfasted and now there's breakfast for your party in the kitchen. Then I think Mr Cameron is keen to get on his way."

Caitlin sat up. On one side of her, Edward stirred and opened his eyes. On her other side, Lynette was concealed under her blankets and there was no movement to suggest she was awake.

"Yes, right, thank you," Caitlin said.

It took quite a lot of poking and persuading to get Lynette to move. Caitlin and Edward had both got their sweaters, socks and shoes back on, rolled up their bedding and been to use the privy before Lynette had so much as sat up.

"It feels really early," she said, pulling on her sweatshirt. She ran her hands through her hair. "I wish I had a hairbrush," she said. Then an expression of horror crossed her face. "Oh no, I need to go to the toilet. I don't want to use that privy place again. It's horrid. No flush and it stinks. It's as bad as having to go behind a bush."

"You could use the pot," Caitlin said, smiling, knowing this would horrify Lynette even more.

"What? No way!" Lynette said. "I want a proper toilet, a

shower, some toothpaste and a toothbrush, and some clean clothes. Is that too much to ask?" she said, tying her laces.

"Yes, it is," Edward said. "You'll have to wait until we get home to get all those things."

"I wish we *were* home. I wish I could have a shower and get clean clothes. I wish I had my hair straighteners. I wish we'd never gone to the Hermitage. I don't care about my bike or who took it. It was a stupid idea. A stupid, stupid..." She kicked her bedding and rubbed at the tears which rolled down her face.

"Lynette—" Caitlin began.

But Lynette pushed past her. "I'm going to the stinking toilet!" she shouted, as she left the room.

"Oh, dear," Caitlin said, looking at Edward.

But Edward just began folding up Lynette's bedding. "She'll get over it," he said.

Lynette was already sitting at the kitchen table when Edward and Caitlin went through. She seemed to have recovered and looked quite happy sitting beside and chatting to Ewen. Caitlin and Edward sat down opposite them. Murdo and the men were sitting at the other end of the table, tucking into bowls of porridge.

"So, do all the Lowlander young folk, even the lassies wear these blue trews?" Ewen asked Lynette, as he glanced over at Edward and Caitlin.

"Trews?" Lynette said.

Ewen nodded downwards, in the direction of Lynette's legs.

"Oh, these. Jeans, you mean?" Lynette replied. "Yes, a lot of us do, not at school of course, there we wear uniform. Some old people wear them too. Caitlin's dad does, the weekends. Though not Edward's dad. He's too posh for that."

Ewen shook his head. He looked mystified. "I see," he said in a voice that showed he really didn't.

Caitlin tried to catch Lynette's eye. She wanted to signal

to her not to say too much about the twenty-first century, but Lynette wouldn't look at her.

Mrs Baxter, the cook, appeared from a doorway at the other side of the kitchen. She was dressed similarly to Mrs Crawford but she had a much bigger apron. She carried two wooden bowls full of porridge which she put down in front of Lynette and Ewen.

"There's plenty of salt in it. And the cream's fresh from the cow," Mrs Baxter said. "It'll set you up for your journey." She smiled at Caitlin and Edward. "I'll just go and fetch yours."

Caitlin thought there was something reassuring, almost familiar about Mrs Baxter's smile.

Ewen began eating immediately, but Lynette just looked in horror at the plate in front of her. "I'm not eating that," she said. "I don't do breakfast."

"We've got a long walk this morning," Caitlin said. "You better have something to give you energy."

Lynette rolled her eyes. "You sound like my mum. She's always banging on about how important breakfast is. I like to get crisps and a Mars bar on the way to school, you know that."

"Well, you can't do that here," Caitlin whispered. "I don't think they had crisps and Mars bars in the eighteenth century."

"They didn't," Edward said.

"I don't suppose they had Coco Pops either," Lynette said, not even trying to keep her voice down.

"Are you going to eat that?" Ewen asked. He'd finished his, and was now looking at Lynette's bowl.

"No," Lynette said, pushing her bowl to him. "You're welcome to it."

Ewen grinned and swapped his empty bowl for Lynette's full one. He began eating right away.

Mrs Baxter returned with porridge for Edward and Caitlin and piled up the empty bowls. "My you're a fast eater," she said to Lynette, smiling.

As she watched Mrs Baxter tidying the table, Caitlin glimpsed a ring on one of the cook's fingers—a large amber ring. Like Mrs Baxter herself, it seemed familiar. It couldn't be, could it?

But Caitlin didn't have time to wonder as the cook's voice broke into her thoughts. "Come on, eat up quickly like your friend," Mrs Baxter said.

The porridge was much saltier and the milk much creamier than Caitlin was used to, but she ate it anyway. It also felt strange to be eating from a wooden bowl and with a wooden spoon. So much was strange. Again she thought of Bella and again she wondered just how much Bella knew, and how. Edward ate in silence, an expression of determination on his face.

"All right, Ed?" Caitlin asked.

"Mmm," he replied, nodding.

"Porridge okay?"

"Yes. We must eat to be ready to walk. So I'm eating."

"Are you sure we're doing the right thing?" Lynette asked, this time lowering her voice. "Don't you think we should be trying to find our own way home?"

"I don't know," Caitlin said. "But it feels safer to be with Murdo and Ewen than to be on our own."

"They said they'd help us," Edward said. "So they will."

Caitlin smiled at Edward. His unwavering, logical way of thinking which could sometimes be so frustrating to deal with, was proving to be very reassuring in their present circumstances. "Yes," she said. "We have to stick to the plan." But deep down she was worried and she shared Lynette's doubts.

It was while they were all eating bacon and eggs, washed down with very strong, strange-tasting tea that Mr Fraser came into the kitchen.

After saying good morning to them all, he turned to

Murdo. "Is it still your plan to walk to Kingussie today?" he asked.

"Yes, I intend to be at the barracks by five this afternoon," Murdo replied.

"The other soldiers, ten in all, and the walking wounded who also spent the night here, they will walk with you, if you're in agreement. And there's a favour I would ask of you," Mr Fraser said.

"And what is that?" Murdo asked.

"There's a young man, son of Chisholm, the Laird down at Kincraig, he was badly hurt, but it seems he'll recover. Now he needs to get home. He can be carried by his comrades. His presence won't slow you down. But I'd be easier in my own mind if I could put him under the protection of someone like yourself, someone I know I can trust."

Caitlin looked at Lynette. She knew her friend was thinking the same as she was. Could it be?

"Chisholm, you say," Murdo said. "They fought bravely, I can't deny that. And it makes sense for us all to travel together, safety in numbers. Are there any officers amongst these men?"

Mr Fraser smiled. "Nobody who outranks you, Murdo, you'd still be in charge."

Murdo nodded. "So, it seems I have two young men to return to their fathers." He glanced at Ewen. "I'll see to it that young Chisholm gets home."

"Good," Mr Fraser said. "Come to the drawing-room when you've finished eating and you can all meet each other before you set off."

The drawing-room was a large space. There was a fire burning in the grate at the far end and all the furniture, sofas, chairs, and small tables, had been pushed to the sides. On the floor were piles of rolled up bedding. There were about twenty men in the room, all dressed in the kilts and over-the-shoulder blankets that already seemed so familiar to

Caitlin and her friends. Some stood talking together. Others sat alone. Several of them had obviously been injured. One man, his head bandaged, stared silently out of the window.

Caitlin didn't spot him immediately. It was only after she had looked around the drawing-room at all the other soldiers that her attention was drawn to the sofa in the corner. A young man lay there, covered by a blanket, his face pale, his eyes closed.

"Angus!" Caitlin cried, rushing across the room. She was sure it was him.

One of the soldiers caught hold of her, his arm round her neck, before she could get to the young man. The sleeve of his coat felt very rough against Caitlin's face. "Where do you think you're going, laddie?" he said.

Caitlin heard Lynette gasp. Murdo laughed out loud. Edward marched over to her side.

"Another laddie!" the soldier said. "Come to rescue your friend?" He laughed.

"I'm not a boy!" said Caitlin, trying to wriggle out of the soldier's grasp.

"Lowland lass," Murdo said. "Harmless." He laughed again.

"Ah, a Lowlander," the soldier said.

"Let her go," Edward said. "Let Caitlin go."

But the soldier just laughed some more.

"Caitlin, Caitlin. Is it you?" The young man on the sofa, struggled to raise his head. "Let her go, Hector," he said. "This is the girl who saved my life."

Hector, the soldier, looked at Caitlin, and then at Angus, in disbelief. "A lassie, a Lowland lassie, saved your life?"

"Yes, yes she did," Angus said. "Now let her go." He sank back against the pillow.

The soldier released Caitlin. She ran over to Angus and knelt at the side of the sofa.

"You're alive," she said. "I'm so glad you're alive."

"Thanks to you," Angus said and he took hold of her hand and squeezed it.

Murdo came over to stand beside them. "Murdo Cameron," he said, looking down at Angus. "We're going to make sure you get home. Tonight you'll sleep in your own bed, in your father's house, I promise."

Angus nodded. He was weak and it was clear he was in pain.

"Your wounds, are they bad?" Murdo asked.

"Bad enough. A bayonet in the gut, it's not good," Angus gasped a little as he spoke. "The regimental surgeon has dressed the wound and the blade doesn't seem to have done lasting damage. But if this girl hadn't stopped the blood, I wouldn't be here to say so."

Murdo looked at Caitlin with new respect. Then he turned to address everyone in the room. He introduced himself and his group including the 'young Lowlanders' to the other group of soldiers and explained that they would all be travelling together on the road to Kingussie. "We'll keep to the cover of the Coignafearn Forest at first, follow the drove road. I know all the hiding places. And then we'll come round by the foot of the Cairngorms and Grampians, to young Chisholm's Kincraig, and then on from there to the barracks," he said. Then he asked for volunteers to carry Angus's stretcher.

Mr Fraser joined them while Murdo was speaking. He wished them all well and they thanked him for his hospitality.

"Mrs Baxter and Mrs Crawford have prepared food for your journey," Mr Fraser said to them all. He turned to Caitlin. "The baskets of supplies have been loaded onto your horse. He's been fed and I've supplied more oats for him for the journey. He stands at the front of the house ready for you, as does your terrier, who, I might add, enjoyed a tasty chicken carcass for his breakfast."

"Thank you so much," Caitlin said.

"And Mrs Crawford has put together some fresh dressings and cloths and some herbs from the apothecary for young Chisholm's wound. From what I hear, you best be responsible for them." He handed a leather pouch to Caitlin.

"Right," Murdo said. "Everybody pick up your packs and let's move out."

Once outside, everyone lined up in pairs, with Angus and his bearers in the middle of the line. Jack Russell, who'd been sitting under the small tree, yelped and bounded up to the children as soon as he saw them, his little tail hard wagging hard. Hero pawed the ground and whinnied on seeing Caitlin and she hugged his head. Edward was to ride him for the first part of the journey and Ewen gave him a hand up into the saddle, as the girls looked on.

Ewen turned to Caitlin and Lynette. He must have seen the strain and apprehension on their faces because he said, "We'll be with my father by day's end today. He'll know how to get you home, don't worry."

It was a pleasant spring morning. The air was filled with birdsong and somewhere in the distance sheep bleated.

Mr Fraser stood on the front step of the house and took out his pocket watch. "Ten o'clock," he said. "You should be at the barracks by five o'clock this afternoon. Farewell, my friends."

Ewen and Lynette walked together behind Hero, and Caitlin decided to walk beside Angus. She thought this was best as she had the medical bag. The stretcher bearers were Hector and another soldier who introduced himself as Norman. Hector and Norman had teased Murdo about how they'd beaten him in getting from the battlefield to Clachmile. They said they'd overtaken Murdo's group on the drove road and said that if they—Hector and Norman—had been Redcoats, then Murdo's group would not have survived. But Murdo had just laughed and said he knew they'd been overtaken and that he'd heard and seen their party, but let them go because he knew they were harmless. Caitlin wasn't sure who to believe but was glad that their small group was now bigger. She'd forgiven Hector for grabbing hold of her so roughly and she liked how he and Norman laughed and how brave they seemed. And both the men, though very strong, were also gentle in their stretcher-bearing task and Angus was soon asleep.

Not far outside Clachmile, they entered the forest. The resiny smell of the pine trees and the way the light filtered through the branches as little birds flitted to and fro reminded Caitlin of the Hermitage. She suddenly felt very homesick. Tears came to her eyes. She missed her father and her brother and sister. She even missed Bella. She reached into the pocket of her jeans and brought out Bella's note. She re-read it, but was no nearer to understanding what it meant. As she put the note back in her pocket a goldfinch flew past her head and landed on a nearby branch. It cocked its head and seemed to look her in the eye as it chirped its cheerful song. For some reason Caitlin felt better.

After a few hours, Murdo signalled for everyone to stop. They were in a bit of a clearing and a small burn ran past where they stood. "We should rest and eat before leaving the forest."

"Thank goodness," Lynette said. "I'm starving and I don't think I could have walked another step. My feet are so sore."

"Mine too," Caitlin said.

When the bread and cheese lunch had been shared out, Caitlin, Edward and Lynette sat together on a large boulder at the side of the clearing. Hero had taken a long drink from the burn and now had a bag of oats to enjoy. Jack had gone scurrying off, no doubt to forage for something of his own to eat. Angus hadn't wanted anything to eat, but Caitlin had helped him take a drink of ale. The ale looked and smelt like a watery version of the beer Caitlin's big brother liked to drink.

"Do you really think Ewen's father will be able to help us?" Lynette asked a little while later, as they ate.

"I hope he can, Caitlin said, "but we'll have to get him to believe us first. I mean it's going to sound pretty strange. '*Hi, we're from the twenty-first century. We slipped back in time by accident and now we need to get back. Can you show us how to do that please?*' Caitlin sighed.

"And even if he's not freaked out by that, how on earth will he be able to send us back?" Lynette said.

"It'll be fine," Edward said. "Bella's note said that we're meant to be here and that we don't need to worry. And didn't it say that we'll go home when the time is right?"

"Yes, yes it did," Caitlin said.

"And speaking of the note, what was all that she said about a quest and that she was watching us?" Lynette said.

"I presume that the quest is the reason we're here," Caitlin said.

"But how are we meant to know what it is? And where's Bella if she's watching over us?" Lynette said.

"She must either be hiding," Edward said, "but then why wouldn't she just come and tell us if she was? Or she has some way of observing us from our own time. But whatever it means, she says *Caitlin* has to fulfill the quest. Bella can't help with that."

"So, where does that leave us?" Lynette asked.

Edward thought for a moment and then he said, "I think we should tell Ewen and Angus who we really are. Bella says in the note to trust friends old *and new* to help."

"What do you think?" Lynette said, turning to Caitlin.

"Hmm, maybe," Caitlin said.

"I agree with Ed," Lynette said. "We're going to have to tell Ewen's father the whole truth and it seems like Angus's father's an important man too. He might also be able to help if we tell him what's happened. And so, getting the boys on our side first would probably be a good idea."

Caitlin could see this made sense. "Okay," she said. "Let's tell Ewen and Angus everything."

"Good," Lynette said. She stood up. "Right, I need a wee." And as she walked away to find a bush to go behind, she added, "There are times when I wish I was a boy!"

Chapter Thirteen

When Lynette came back over to them, Edward said, "I'll go and talk to Ewen. You two go and sit by Angus, he's on his own at the moment. I'll get Ewen to come with me and join you."

Angus's stretcher was under a tree. A makeshift pillow, made from someone's rolled up tartan blanket was placed against the trunk, so he could lean back and sit with some support. He smiled when he saw the girls and Jack approaching.

Caitlin noticed that he had more colour in his face than he'd had earlier. "How are you feeling?" she asked, as she and Lynette sat down on the grass beside him.

"I'm feeling a bit better," he said. "The pain isn't so bad."

"Would you like me to put on a fresh dressing?" Caitlin asked.

"Good idea," Angus said. He pulled the blanket back and lifted his shirt.

Caitlin took a pad of soft cloth and a long strip of cotton from the leather pouch. She also took some of the herbs out of the side pocket. She gave them to Lynette to hold.

Angus leaned forward and Caitlin gently unwound the bandage and removed the dressing. The wound looked clean, the skin had already started knitting together and there was no sign of any blood on the pad. It didn't take her long to re-dress the injury.

"Thanks," Angus said when she'd finished. "You're better

than the army surgeon."

"My father's a doctor," she said, blushing at the compliment.

"Is he?"Angus said. "Is he an army surgeon or a physician?"

"He's a GP," Caitlin said. "At the medical centre."

"What's a GP? And what's a medical centre?"

"It's a place where doctors work. A GP is a doctor you go to if what's wrong with you isn't serious enough for hospital. I don't think you—that is—there weren't—or there aren't…" Caitlin wasn't sure how to begin to explain what she meant.

"The thing is," Edward said as he and Ewen arrived, "there's no such thing as a GP in the eighteenth century. "And you and Ewen live in the eighteenth century, so that's why you don't know what one is."

"Uh, but *you* know what it is, and you live in the eighteenth century too," Angus said and Ewen sniggered.

Lynette whispered to Caitlin, "They're never going to believe us."

"That's just it," Edward said. "We don't. Lynette, Caitlin and I, we live in the twenty-first century. Where we come from it's not 1746, it's 2014.

Ewen and Angus exchanged glances.

"I thought you said you were from Edinburgh?" Angus said, looking at Caitlin.

"We are. But we're also from the future," Caitlin said.

"We know it sounds crazy," Lynette said. "But we're telling the truth."

"So how did you get here? How did you travel back more than two hundred years?" Ewen asked. He grinned at Angus and shook his head in disbelief.

"We're not sure," Caitlin said. "We were at a park in Edinburgh. We were hiding near an ice house trying to catch the people who'd stolen our bikes. We leant on an old pine tree and the next thing we knew we were falling backwards down some sort of tunnel. We landed beside you."

"What's bikes?" Ewen asked.

"A park? An ice house?" Angus asked.

Caitlin, Lynette and Edward looked at each other. This really wasn't going to be easy.

"Look," Caitlin said, scrabbling in her bag for her phone. "It may not have a signal," she said to Edward and Lynette, but there's still just enough battery that I can get my photos." She found a picture she'd taken of her bike. She turned the screen towards Ewen and Angus. "That's a bike," she said.

They peered at the screen, looking even more puzzled.

"What does it do, this bike thing?" Ewen asked.

"You ride it. It takes you where you want to go," Lynette said. She pointed at the screen. "These things are pedals. You push them with your feet while you're sitting on the saddle and the bike rolls forward."

"Like a horse, but with wheels?" Ewen asked.

"Yes – sort of," Lynette said.

"Never mind that," Angus said. He was now sitting right up. "What is that?" He pointed at the phone.

Caitlin laughed. "That's a phone with a camera in it."

Angus and Ewen just looked at her blankly.

"It's a thing you can use to communicate, to speak to people far away," Caitlin said. "And it also takes photos. That is it catches a picture of what you're looking at it and keeps it."

Angus nodded, slowly. Ewen still looked baffled.

"I'll show you," Caitlin said. She waved a hand at Ewen. "Crouch down beside Angus and both of you look at me." Angus and Ewen did as they'd been told. Caitlin pointed her phone and clicked. "Look," she said, turning the phone screen towards them.

Ewen grabbed the phone. "What? How? That's..." He shook his head and handed the phone to Angus.

Angus didn't say anything at first. He didn't have to. His

amazement was obvious. He gazed at the photo for a long moment, before handing the phone back to Caitlin. "There is magic here I don't understand. But somehow our portrait has been painted inside that tiny box." He was quiet again for a minute. Then he said, "And with it you could also communicate with my father, or Ewen's?"

"No, they would need one of these as well, and there's no signal here, in the eighteenth century."

"Signal?" Angus said.

But before Caitlin could even begin to explain that one, Murdo called to them that it was time to move. Hector and Norman began making their way over to pick up Angus's stretcher. "We'll talk more later, at my father's house," Angus whispered to Caitlin.

Caitlin and Lynette rode Hero; Lynette's need for a break from walking having overcome her stubbornness about getting on the horse. She sat behind Caitlin and held on tightly, and she only complained for a short time. Edward and Jack walked with Ewen. It wasn't long before they left the cover of the forest and emerged on to the drove road. To the east, the Cairngorm Mountains ranged along the horizon, snow still on the tops. And to the south of them, the Grampians stretched into the distance.

It was probably around four in the afternoon when the group approached the edge of Kincraig. Ahead of Caitlin and her friends, Murdo raised his hand in the air, signaling everyone to stop. As she pulled on Hero's reins, Caitlin saw one of Murdo's men coming towards them. He stopped when he got to Caitlin.

"Miss," the man said. "It seems Master Chisholm wants to talk to you. You're to come right away."

"Right," Caitlin said. She glanced over her shoulder at Lynette. "I'll need to dismount."

"Just as I was getting used to this," Lynette said.

Murdo's man helped both the girls down. Edward took

Hero's reins and Caitlin went to see Angus. The stretcher was on the ground and Angus was leaning on one of the bearers and getting to his feet when she walked up to him.

"I have another favour to ask of you, Caitlin," Angus said. "We're near to my home and I do not want to be carried to my father's door. I want to walk up and I want you at my side when I do." He straightened up and let go of the man supporting him. He winced as he did so and beckoned to Caitlin. She went and stood alongside him. He was a good bit taller than Caitlin, about her brother's height. He leant one arm along her shoulder and clutched his wound with his free hand. Caitlin slid her arm behind his back and held on to his shirt. Slowly and warily they began to walk. Murdo signalled to everyone else to move.

After about twenty or thirty metres they arrived at the gates of Kincraig House. Angus was home. Caitlin felt his body shudder. She looked up at him. Tears trickled down his face. He saw her looking. His hand flew from his wound and he rubbed at the tears.

"It's all right to cry," Caitlin whispered to him. And a memory of her father saying the same thing to James when their mum died came into her head. She swallowed hard. She also realised it was what people kept saying to her as well.

"I'm not crying. I never cry," Angus whispered back and Caitlin smiled.

"What are you smiling at?" Angus hissed.

"You sound just like my big brother," Caitlin replied.

Murdo marched up and stood in front of them and rattled the gates. They were locked. "Hello!" Murdo called. "Chisholm, are you there? Hello."

Caitlin leaned as far as she could round Murdo's back, and peered through the gate and up the driveway towards the grey-stone house. A face appeared at one of the few unshuttered windows. Murdo clattered at the gates and called out again.

After a minute, an elderly man in a kilt came walking down the driveway towards them.

He frowned at Murdo as he drew near. "What is it? What's all the shouting? Who are you? What do you want?" He looked round at Murdo and his men and the soldiers standing behind them.

"Murdo Cameron. Please open the gates and let us in. We're no threat. We fought on the moor for the Prince. We're on our way back to the barracks, but first I must see the Laird, Mr Chisholm. I have – I have something for him."

"The Laird isn't seeing anyone," the man said. "He's in mourning."

"Mourning?" Murdo said. "For whom, may I ask?"

"For his son, young Angus, his heir, killed on Culloden field."

"Angus, you say?" Murdo said, a smile twitching at his mouth.

Then Angus called out, "Kenneth, Kenneth, it's me. Open the gates!" He and Caitlin stepped out from behind the men.

"Angus, oh my word, Angus!" A key was turned in the lock and the gates flung open.

Angus, let go of Caitlin and walked forward to greet the old man. The two of them embraced and exchanged a few words and then Kenneth started walking back towards the house.

Angus beckoned to the others. "Come," he said. "Come to the house. Come and meet my father."

By the time the party had made their way up the drive, Kenneth had reappeared with another man, a man who looked so like Angus that he had to be his father. The man, wearing a tweed jacket and kilt in the same tartan as Kenneth's ran down the steps towards them. He was followed by a woman, a small woman in a long blue dress, with a white shawl around her shoulders. She also ran down the steps, her arms outstretched. "Angus, oh, Angus!" she cried.

Angus stepped forward and limped into his mother's arms. Caitlin couldn't be certain, but she was fairly sure that it wasn't just her who cried as they witnessed the reunion of mother, father and son.

After some moments, Angus's father addressed them all. "Thank you to all of you. Thank you for bringing my son home to me."

Angus looked very happy. He stood slightly awkwardly - partly because of his wound, and partly because his mother had not released him from her embrace. He glanced over at Caitlin and then spoke to his parents.

After a few moments, Angus's father called out, "Miss Cameron, Miss Cameron from Edinburgh." He held out his hand towards Caitlin. She blushed and looked at the ground. Lynette pushed her in the back. She stumbled forward and took the outstretched hand. "Thank you, Miss Cameron, thank you." Angus's father spoke softly, his voice cracking, as he shook her hand. His grip was warm and strong.

Caitlin looked into his eyes, eyes that were very like those of his son, eyes that had tears in them, eyes that looked at her so kindly. She smiled at him, unsure of what to say.

Angus's mother meanwhile had let go of her son and she too stepped forward to greet Caitlin. She took both of Caitlin's hands in hers. "I hear that it was you who saved Angus, you that stopped to tend to him when you could have walked past, and you who knew what to do. I can never thank you enough, never repay what you have done for us." Then she let go of Caitlin's hands and hugged her. "If there is ever anything we can do for you, you have only to ask."

"Indeed so," Angus's father said. Then he turned to the others. "You are all most welcome here. You must come in and have some refreshment before you journey on." He beckoned to them all. "Please, please come in."

Kenneth took Hero's reins from Edward and led him away to be given food and water. And the group, including Jack, all followed Mr Chisholm indoors. This house was grander than Mr Fraser's. They stepped through the front door into a Great Hall. The Hall was galleried and at least twice as big as the one at Fraser's place. Fires burned in the grates of the fireplaces at either end. Large paintings of kilted men hung on the walls. Caitlin guessed they must be Angus's ancestors.

Everyone found somewhere to sit, on sofas, chairs and floor rugs, and Mr Chisholm excused himself. Caitlin and Lynette shared one footstool and Ewen and Edward another. Jack curled up at Caitlin's feet. Angus, who'd gone very pale and looked exhausted, was taken away by his mother to be put to bed. Caitlin watched them go. She remembered how her own mother used to look after her when she was ill. How she'd stroke her hair and... But then her mother had got ill herself. Caitlin sighed, swallowed hard, bit her lip, fought the lump of sadness. Jack put his paw on her leg and she patted his head. Then she felt Lynette's hand on hers, squeezing it.

"Are you okay?" Lynette whispered.

"Yes, no—not really," Caitlin whispered back. "I was just missing my mum, you know?"

Lynette nodded and squeezed Caitlin's hand again. "I know."

Caitlin rested her head on her Lynette's shoulder and held her hand tightly for a few moments.

It wasn't long before Mr Chisholm returned and with him came several servants with platefuls of food and jugs of ale and blackcurrant juice. The food and drink were laid out on a long narrow table in a corner at the back of the hall and Mr Chisholm told them all to help themselves.

One of the servants, a tall young woman in a white cap, long dress and apron, stopped to turn and smile at Caitlin, Edward and Lynette before departing. As with Mrs Baxter, the cook at Fraser's place, Caitlin thought there was something familiar about the woman's smile.

On the table there was chicken and ham, bread and

cheese, apples and cake. And even although it was only a couple of hours since they'd last eaten, everyone was already hungry from the walking, and so they all loaded up their plates.

Mr Chisholm talked to Murdo while they ate. He no doubt wanted news of how the battle had gone, and of Mr Fraser, and to thank Murdo for his part in bringing Angus home.

Caitlin had just finished eating, when the servant who'd smiled at her and her two friends, came back into the hall.

She came over to Caitlin. "Mr Angus would like to see you, miss," she said. "I'm to take you up."

"Oh, right," said Caitlin. She looked at Lynette and Edward. Edward just carried on eating, but Lynette smiled at her.

"Go on," Lynette said. "He probably wants to thank you one last time before we go."

Caitlin followed the servant up a flight of stairs and along a passageway to a door.

Before she knocked on the door, the servant turned to Caitlin and patted her on the arm. "You mustn't worry. Angus and Ewen will both help you, as will their fathers. You will find out your purpose and you *will* get home."

Caitlin was puzzled. "How did you, how do you—"

"Shh," the young woman said, shaking her head and knocking on the door. "Trust me." She opened the door and gestured for Caitlin to go in ahead of her.

Angus was propped up in a bed near the window. "Thanks, Izzie," he said.

Caitlin glanced back at the servant. The woman smiled again and Caitlin felt the same feeling of reassurance she'd got from Mrs Baxter. Then Izzie was gone, closing the door behind her.

Angus pointed to the chair beside his bed. "Sit down," he said.

Caitlin did as he asked.

"You'll be leaving for the barracks soon," Angus said.

Caitlin nodded. She couldn't meet Angus's eye. She looked down at the floor, studied the grain of the wooden the floorboards. Part of her was desperate to be on her way, to be getting nearer to getting home, but another part of her was sad about saying goodbye to Angus.

"Caitlin?" Angus leant forward, trying to look into her face. "Caitlin, what is it? What's wrong?"

She sighed and looked up at him. "I don't want to say goodbye. I want to know you're going to be all right, and I'll miss you, but I also want to go home."

Angus smiled at her. "I'll miss you too. But you mustn't worry about me. I'm much better. I'm going to be fine, thanks to you. We'll always be friends. I know we will."

"What, even after I get home, *if* I get home? Even if we're two hundred miles and two hundred and seventy years apart?"

"Yes, even then," Angus said. "I can't explain. I don't understand any more than you do, but I don't think this is over yet. I feel sure we'll meet again. There's a reason you and your friends arrived here. I think you'll find that reason with Ewen's father."

"I hope you're right," Caitlin said.

Chapter Fourteen

Edward rode Hero for the remainder of the journey to Kingussie. It was late afternoon when they arrived. Caitlin felt as if she'd been away from home for days. It was hard to believe that it was only yesterday that she'd been in the Hermitage. She wondered how her dad would be feeling. What if Bella's note was wrong? What if she was being missed? Her father would be frantic and so would Lynette and Edward's families. And how could Bella be right? It didn't make any sense.

Ewen's voice broke in on Caitlin's thoughts. He'd walked beside her and Lynette all the way from Kincraig. "This is the barracks," he said, as Murdo banged on the big wooden door in the middle of the high wall.

A sentry peered through a hatch in the door and while Murdo explained who they were, Edward dismounted and, still holding Hero's reins, came to stand beside Lynette, Ewen and Caitlin. Ewen was excited and impatient to get inside.

"Do you think your father will be here?" Edward asked.

"Murdo certainly thinks so," Ewen said, peering round Edward to watch the door. "It was where my father ordered his men to take him as soon as he was injured. He knew the Redcoats wanted him dead. Cameron of Locheil, leader of the biggest clan on the battlefield, would be a great prize for them. So once he was hurt he had to get away, and he knew he'd be safe here. "

There was the sound of bars and bolts being drawn back and the door to the barracks creaked open at last. Sentries stood either side of the doorway as Murdo's party entered. A man with the same wild red hair as Ewen, and dressed in a kilt of the same Cameron tartan, appeared from a low building at the back of the courtyard where the party now stood.

"Murdo," the man called. He embraced Murdo and the two men talked quietly together as the others looked on.

"My uncle," Ewen said to Edward and the girls. He was dancing from foot to foot with impatience.

After a few minutes, Murdo turned and beckoned to Ewen.

The man stepped forward to meet his nephew. "Young Ewen," he said. "Thank God." "Your father will be relieved you are safe." The man stood with his hands on Ewen's shoulders and smiled at him.

"Where is he, Uncle? Is he all right? I must go to him," Ewen said.

The man's face fell. "He was here only briefly, I'm afraid. His wounds were dressed and then, at nightfall he was carried from here. God willing, he'll be home at Achnaharrie by now."

"He's gone! Already? Why? Why didn't he wait for me? No, you must be mistaken. He would have waited!" Ewen stepped past his uncle. "Father!" he shouted. "Father, where are you?"

Ewen's uncle caught hold of Ewen's arm and pulled him round to face him. "He wanted to wait, but he daren't. We heard the Redcoats were in pursuit and we knew if there were enough of them they could take the barracks and Locheil would be shown no mercy. More of our men have arrived today. Many of them Lowlanders on their way south. They say the King's men have retaken Inverness and that Butcher Cumberland's troops slaughtered any of our Highlanders they met on the way."

"The Redcoats turned back to Inverness before Kincraig,"

Ewen said. "You'd have been safe. He'd have been safe. He should have stayed."

"We weren't to know the enemy wouldn't be coming."

Ewen's shoulders drooped and his head went down as he saw the sense of what his uncle had told him.

His uncle smiled kindly at him and put an arm round his shoulders. "It was better that your father got away. We must hope the Redcoats assume him to be dead, at least until he is fit again. Another day's travel and you'll be reunited at Achnaharrie."

Ewen nodded. "I suppose so," he said.

"But now, introduce me to your young friends," said his uncle. "And then we'll get everyone settled in for the night."

After the introductions, Hero was led away to the stables by one of Ewen's uncle's men and the weary group were ushered into the grey-stone building at the far side of the entrance courtyard.

Once inside, Ewen's uncle led them all into a large room, which reminded Caitlin of the dining hall at school. Lots of men sat at long narrow tables, men dressed like Ewen and Murdo, some with bloodstained shirts. They glanced up from their food as the group entered. Their faces were as weary as those of the new arrivals and they quickly got back to eating, too tired to be curious.

Ewen's uncle took them to the serving table, where two women stood behind several, enormous, cauldron-like cooking pots. The women handed them each a tin plate and then they were all given a few dollops of, what looked like, one of Caitlin's granny's stews.

Murdo and his men along with Ewen, Caitlin, Lynette and Edward sat together at one table. The soldiers, who'd come with them from Fraser's place, went off to seek out comrades at the other tables. Caitlin's group ate in almost complete silence. They were too hungry and too tired for talk. Caitlin shared some of her stew with Jack who sat under the table at her feet.

"That was the best rabbit stew, ever!" Ewen said as he finished his last mouthful.

Edward nodded in agreement. Caitlin kept on eating, but looked at Lynette. Lynette paused, her spoon halfway to her mouth. Then she shrugged and kept on eating. Caitlin laughed.

"What?" Lynette said.

"You've changed! You're eating a cute wee bunny! "Caitlin said.

"Yeah, yeah," Lynette said. "I'm having to do a lot of stuff I never thought I could."

"Mmm," Caitlin said, nodding, serious now. "I think we all are."

After their meal, Ewen's uncle came to show them where they would be sleeping that night. Murdo and the men would be in one of the main barrack rooms. Caitlin, Lynette and the boys were in a small room off the main room. Before they parted for the night, Murdo told them that they would need to be up early in the morning for the final part of their journey to Achnaharrie.

On the floor of their little room, there were four rolled-up tartan blankets made of coarse wool. Caitlin and her two friends made makeshift pillows from their sweatshirts and Ewen rolled up his plaid to rest his head on.

Then they all lay down on the floor and rolled their blankets around them. Through the little window high up in the wall, they could see that it was just starting to get dark outside.

The children lay side by side. Ewen and Edward were by the door and the girls were under the window with Jack lying in between them. Although they were tired, they all found it difficult to fall asleep. And it wasn't just the hardness of the floor that was preventing them from sleeping.

"So, do you think we'll get home tomorrow?" Lynette

asked, turning on her side and speaking softly to Caitlin.

"I don't know," Caitlin said. "Angus said he was sure that we'd get some answers from Ewen's father."

Ewen propped himself up on one elbow as the girls spoke. "Angus also seemed sure you had ended up here for a reason," he said. "He was going on about how it was meant that you arrived to save him." Ewen still sounded like he didn't fully believe the twenty-first century story.

Edward sat up, pulling his blanket around him. "It doesn't matter to me if it was meant or not, I just want to get home," he said.

"Me too," Lynette said.

"And me," Caitlin said.

"Yeah, well wherever, and whenever, you're from, if anyone can get you back there, it's my father," Ewen said. "But right now, I think we should all try to get some sleep."

Chapter Fifteen

It was around three o'clock in the afternoon when they arrived at the gates of Achnaharrie. Lynette and Edward had ridden Hero for the first half of the journey from the barracks, and then Caitlin rode him for the rest of the way. She slid down off the horse's back as Murdo rattled the locked and chained gates.

Ewen ran up beside Murdo. He too rattled the gates. "Father," he called. "Father, it's me, Ewen. Your son is home. Let us in."

Nobody was prepared for what happened next. Murdo and Ewen jumped back from the gates. Their hands up. A small cloaked figure had appeared from the bushes at the side of the driveway and was now pointing a musket at Ewen's chest.

"So, you're home and now every Redcoat for miles around knows it!" the musket bearer said, sweeping back the hood of the cloak. "Am I going to have to shoot you to get you to shut up?"

Ewen gasped and Murdo laughed.

"Well, I'll be—" Murdo said

"Lucy!" Ewen shouted. "What are you doing? Put the musket down and let us in."

Caitlin stared at the person on the other side of the gate. It was a girl, a girl about Caitlin's age.

The girl glowered at Ewen. "You're lucky I wasn't a Redcoat. I could have blown your head off." She laid down the gun and reached under her cloak. She produced a bunch of keys and quickly unchained and unlocked the gates. "Hurry," she said beckoning the party to come inside.

As soon as they'd all gone through, she closed and re-locked the entrance. Then she flung her arms round Ewen's neck. "Thank God, you're still alive. We didn't know. We thought the Redcoats might have got you on the road. Father has been so worried."

Ewen hugged her tightly. "How is he? How is Father?" he asked, as he stepped back from her.

Lucy frowned. "He's in a lot of pain and he can't walk. But he's going to be so pleased to see you. And you too, Murdo, and all your men, and..." She paused, looking over at Caitlin, Lynette and Edward. "And these people—"

"Lowlanders, from the battle, he's a drummer, not that I actually saw him with a drum, now I come to think of it," Ewen said. "The girls are attendants to the sick and injured, I think. Anyway they need Father's help to get home."

"I see." Lucy stepped forward. "I'm Lucy, Ewen's sister. I'm pleased to meet you." She held out her hand to Caitlin.

Lynette gave a little giggle and murmured, "How old-fashioned is she? She'll be curtseying next."

"Shh," Caitlin said through gritted teeth. "Of course she's old-fashioned! This is the eighteenth century."

Caitlin smiled at Lucy, and grasped her outstretched hand. "I'm Caitlin, Caitlin Cameron and this is Lynette Maclean and Edward Farquharson." As they all shook hands Caitlin looked more closely at Lucy. She had curly auburn hair and her face was covered in freckles.

"She looks like you," Lynette whispered to Caitlin.

"I was just thinking that," Caitlin replied.

Edward got all flustered as he shook Lucy's hand and Caitlin was sure he blushed. Lynette noticed too and nudged Caitlin.

"Whose is the horse?" Lucy asked. Hero had followed the

group through the gates and was now nibbling at a hedge by the side of the driveway.

"Ah, well that's a long story, " Ewen replied."He sort of adopted us after some Redcoats abandoned him on the road."

"He's a beauty," Lucy said going over to him. She patted his neck and he nuzzled her hand. She leant in against him and said "Ah," as if the horse had said something to her.

Caitlin and Lynette exchanged a glance. Lynette raised her eyebrows and shrugged.

"He's called Hero," Caitlin said. "At least, that's what *we* named him."

Lucy nodded. "Yes, I thought so. He can be taken round to the stables. The stable lad will feed him and put him in a stall."

Murdo nodded to one of the men, who led Hero away.

Then Lucy noticed Jack peeping out from behind Caitlin's legs. "And who's this?" she asked bending to pat the little dog.

"This is Jack Russell," said Caitlin.

"Ah," Lucy said, then added, "Now, come, we should get inside.

"We'll not stay," Murdo said. "I'll just pay my respects to your father, and if he needs nothing more from us today, then me and the men will go to our homes. We all have our own families awaiting our return."

Ewen went in first to see his father. Locheil was in a room off the large square entrance hall where, Lucy explained, a bed had been made up for him after it had proved too difficult to get him up the stairs to his bedroom. Lucy went and sat on a long sofa that stood against the back wall of the hall and she beckoned to Caitlin and Lynette to join her. Edward was wandering around the hall looking at the paintings of Cameron ancestors that hung on the walls and making notes in his notebook. Murdo and the men stood together talking in quiet voices.

After a little while, Ewen came back out to them. He

looked pale and shocked. Lucy went up to him and he put his arm around her shoulder. "He wants to see you, Murdo," he said. "And I'm to tell the men to go home to their wives and children without further delay."

Murdo nodded, and after he'd said goodbye to the men, he went to see Locheil.

Caitlin felt quite sad as she and her friends said their own goodbyes to Hector and Norman and the rest of Murdo's men. It felt like they'd been through a lot together, although it had only been for a short time. The men felt like—what?—friends, or uncles maybe, big brothers perhaps?

"My father is very tired," Ewen said, after the men had gone. "But he wants to meet you three and says he will see you in the morning. He says you're to have dinner here and a bed for the night. It seems, it seems you are who you say you are, and he's been expecting you." He sank down in an armchair and Lucy went and sat on a small stool at his feet.

"Right," Caitlin said, not sure whether to be relieved or not. Edward was still going round the paintings and Lynette was kneeling on the floor playing with Jack. Caitlin looked over at Ewen. He looked so worried and she felt sorry for him. She knew how she would feel if anything happened to her dad. "It must have been a shock," she said, "seeing your father so injured."

"Yes," Ewen replied. "He's normally so strong."

"Is your mother with him?" Caitlin asked.

Ewen shook his head and stared into the fire. It was Lucy who spoke. "Our mother is dead," she said.

"Oh," Caitlin said. She bit her lip.

"Don't be upset," Lucy said. We don't really remember her. She died when I was a baby and Ewen was only two. But it means our father is even more important to us."

"Oh," Caitlin said again and it felt like a great big wave of missing and sadness broke over her head. She let out a little sobbing sound.

Lynette jumped up and came to sit beside Caitlin on the sofa. She put her arm round Caitlin's shoulders.

"I'm sorry," Lucy said. "Please, don't upset yourself on our account."

"Caitlin's mother died too," Lynette said. "It was two years ago. I think what you said, it just made her remember and made her sad."

Lucy nodded. "I see."

Edward came over and sat beside the girls. "I think we are all missing our homes. We need to get back."

Ewen leant forward. "And you will. I know what it is to miss home." He looked at Caitlin and smiled kindly at her. I know what it is to miss the ones you love. My father will get you home. I promise."

When Murdo came out from seeing Ewen's father, he looked very serious. Ewen stood up to meet him and they shook hands. "Thank you," Ewen said. "For bringing me home to my father and for your loyalty."

Murdo nodded and he embraced Ewen and slapped him on the back a couple of times. Then he offered his hand to Edward. "Master Farquharson, it has been good to make your acquaintance."

Edward stood up and shook hands. "And it's been good meeting you. Thanks for bringing us here."

Then Murdo turned to Lynette and Caitlin. "Ladies," he said, smiling at the girls and giving a little bow.

"Goodbye, Murdo," Lynette said. "And thank you for keeping us safe."

"Goodbye, Miss Maclean. You've been a good soldier, for a lassie." He grinned at her and Lynette giggled.

Caitlin couldn't speak because of the pain in her throat. If the men seemed like uncles and brothers, then Murdo was like a father. She ran to him and hugged him.

"Ah, Miss Cameron," Murdo said, surprised and smiling. "It's been a privilege to journey with such a brave young woman. I believe you'll make a fine physician one day. But now I must go home."

After the door had closed behind Murdo, Lucy turned to Caitlin and the others and said, "So, how did you meet Ewen?"

And so, as the afternoon turned to evening, Caitlin, Lynette, Edward and Ewen shared the telling of the story of their meeting.

"I'm so glad you turned up in time to save Angus Chisholm, and I know you're here with us for a reason too," Lucy said.

"Oh, and what is that reason?" asked Caitlin. As she spoke, a woman carrying a basin and a towel appeared and went into Locheil's room.

"Yes," Lynette said. "What do you mean? What reason?"

Lucy opened her mouth to answer. But before she could, Lynette went on, "And what was all that about Hero's name earlier? When you said you thought so, when we told you his name. And what was going on when you seemed to be talking to him, and he seemed to be talking to you? You some kind of horse whisperer?" Lynette gave a slightly mocking laugh.

"There are such people, Lynette," Edward said. "And, as you know, Hero communicates with me. He's definitely a special kind of horse."

"Indeed he is," Lucy said, smiling at Edward. "I just know it."

Edward blushed.

Lynette shook her head. "And you do know that we're not just from Edinburgh, but that we're also from two hundred and sixty-eight years into the future?" she said, looking smug. She clearly thought that Lucy had no idea.

Caitlin, though, wasn't so sure.

Again, Lucy smiled that knowing smile. And she didn't look in the least surprised by what Lynette had just said.

But before Lucy could answer, the woman who'd gone into Locheil's room came back out. She walked over to them smiling.

"Mrs Murray," Ewen said, standing to greet the woman.

"Master Ewen, it's good to have you home."

"Thank you."

"Mr Cameron is so happy that you're safe and back with us. And he tells me we have guests." Mrs Murray beamed at Caitlin and her friends.

"Yes, this is Caitlin, Lynette and Edward and they'll be with us for dinner and overnight."

"I'm Mrs Murray," the woman said. "I look after Mr Cameron and the family. And you're all from Edinburgh, I believe." The children nodded. "My sister's been there, and some of the stories, well..." She laughed, before continuing. "Anyway, you are all most welcome here. Now, I'll go and organise dinner and beds." And with that she bustled off.

"Good," Lucy said. "Now, where were we?"

"I'd just told you that we're from the twenty-first century," Lynette said. "What do you make of that? You didn't know that before, did you?"

"Yes, I did," Lucy said. "You three were one of my first 'sights'. I've sort of been expecting you."

"You have?" Ewen and Lynette said together.

"Since when?" Lynette asked.

"What do you mean sights?" Caitlin asked.

"I think we should let Lucy explain," Edward said.

Lucy smiled her smile at Edward. Lynette rolled her eyes at Caitlin.

"I've known for some time that I have special abilities," Lucy said. "I would get strange feelings, like I wasn't quite in the world, and then I'd be looking at something that I knew wasn't really there. It would be like looking through a window and I'd get a glimpse of something, a person or an object and then it would vanish and everything would go back to normal—until the next time."

"You never said anything," Ewen said.

"I did actually. I mentioned it to Father. And he said not to worry. He said our mother and our grandmother had it too—the sight. It's a way of seeing through time, and it seems I've inherited it from them."

"Why have I not heard of this—this gift?" Ewen asked.

"According to Father, it's not something that's spoken of without good reason. He also said I would grow into it and learn how to use it, and, that until that happened, I should keep it to myself."

"And have you grown into it?" Caitlin asked.

Lucy nodded. "Yes, since my thirteenth birthday, at the beginning of this year, the glimpses have become clearer. I saw Culloden field and a young man, I now know to be Angus, lying injured and Caitlin tending to him. I saw Hero and I saw—I saw all of you."

"You saw us all on the battlefield?" Edward said.

"No, not all of you, at least not on the battlefield, but I did see you all with the Prince, with Bonnie Prince Charlie. You were—well—I shouldn't say what you were doing, not now."

"But we haven't met the Prince," Lynette said. "Not on the battlefield, or on the road."

"Yes, I know," Lucy said. "That's why I shouldn't talk about it. It hasn't happened yet." Lucy glanced anxiously at her brother. Ewen looked shocked by his sister's revelations. "I'm sorry I didn't tell you before," she said. "I hadn't really got used to the idea myself."

The room fell silent as they all thought about what Lucy had just said. The only sound was the grandfather clock in the corner ticking time away.

Caitlin's mind dashed backwards and forwards and round and round. She thought back a couple of days to when she was lying on her bed reading, to the locket in its box and to the conversations she'd had with Bella. She thought about what Lucy had said about meeting the Prince. Did that mean their time here in 1746 really wasn't finished yet? And then she thought about going home, home to her dad and Jamie and Fiona, and telling them about this adventure.

"Dinner's ready." Mrs Murray's cheery voice interrupted everyone's thoughts. "I've set it all up in the kitchen. I thought it would be cosier there than in the dining room. Come on through everybody."

They all stood up, looking around them as if they'd just woken up and weren't sure where they were.

Mrs Murray laughed. "Early nights for everyone, I think. You all look exhausted."

They followed her to the kitchen. Five steaming bowls of broth stood ready on the kitchen table.

"There's venison stew and dumplings to follow," Mrs Murray said. "So sit down and get started."

"Venison?" Lynette said. "What's that?"

Mrs Murray looked surprised. "It's deer, meat from a deer."

Caitlin held her breath. But all Lynette said was, "Right—from a deer—that's okay."

As they settled to eat the soup, Mrs Murray sliced a large loaf of crusty of bread and put it in the middle of the table. "Help yourselves," she said.

"Thank you," Caitlin said. "The soup is very nice. It tastes just like my granny's."

"Does it? That's good!" Mrs Murray smiled at her. Then she looked serious. "Though, I don't know how much longer I can keep making such meals."

"Why not?" Ewen asked.

"Oh, don't listen to me. Eat up and enjoy it. I'll leave the dish of stew and some platters here on the side and perhaps you could serve up, Miss Lucy?"

Lucy nodded.

"Good." Mrs Murray piled plates of food onto a tray as

she spoke. "Now, I must take Mr Cameron his meal and I'll be staying to dine with him. I'll come back later to show our guests to their rooms."

A little while later, as Caitlin and the others, including Lynette, ate their platefuls of stew,

Lynette turned to Lucy and said, "So, from what you said earlier, did you mean we're not going home yet, that we still have to meet Prince Charlie?"

"Yes, I mean no, I—oh, I don't know exactly." Lucy put down her spoon and frowned. "I said already, I don't think I should tell you any more about it. My father will explain, I'm sure."

"But why on earth would we meet the Prince?" Caitlin asked.

Lucy shrugged. "I don't know. Maybe the Prince needs your help."

"Right," Edward said, "so we've been brought back from 2014 to do something for Bonnie Prince Charlie. He must be really special if people have to be brought back from the future to do stuff for him."

"Yeah," Lynette laughed, "And we must be very special too, to be the ones who've been brought back to help, out of all the trillions and zillions of people in the world."

"You're almost right. The Prince is certainly very special," Lucy said. "A lot of Scotland's pride and honour depend on him surviving. A lot of people in Scotland and England want him to be king of Britain. But there are lots of people in both countries who are on the side of King George and his Redcoats and who don't want him as king. The Redcoats are determined to see him off."

"And that's why they're killing anyone who they believe might help the Prince," Ewen said. "Father said that from tomorrow night Murdo and his men are going to take it in turns to guard this house. None of us can be safe until Charlie's safe."

Lynette looked at Lucy. "What did you mean when you said I was *almost* right about us and the Prince being special?"

"Ah, well, I think out of your group, it's Caitlin who's special. I believe it's her who *has* to be here," Lucy said.

"Oh, charming! So me and Edward, we're what, pointless extras?"

"No, not exactly," Lucy said. She was looking more and more uncomfortable. "I think you're here to help her because you're her friends."

"Hmm," Lynette said. "Okay, but—"

"Please!" Lucy raised her hands. "Please stop asking me all these questions. I've said too much already. It's not my role to explain. Speak to my father in the morning. All I do know is there is some special link between Caitlin and Bonnie Prince Charlie."

Chapter Sixteen

Next morning, when Caitlin, Lynette and Edward entered the kitchen, Ewen was already there eating his breakfast. He appeared to be sharing it with Jack who was sitting at his feet. Lucy was helping Mrs Murray bring food to the table.

"Good morning," Mrs Murray said. "Did you sleep well?"

"Yes, thank you," Caitlin replied, speaking for all three of them. She felt it was the polite answer, but she knew it wasn't really true.

They'd all been restless. Caitlin had dreamed strange dreams in which Lucy and Ewen were her brother and sister, and Murdo and her father appeared to be the same person. She knew her friends were as impatient as she was to meet with Ewen's father, and to find out if he did indeed know how they could all get home. She noticed that neither Lynette nor Edward were eating their porridge and she was also finding it difficult to eat.

As if he read their thoughts, Ewen said, "Don't worry. My father will see you after breakfast."

"You've quite a journey ahead of you," Mrs Murray said, looking at them kindly. "You really should eat up."

Caitlin wondered what Mrs Murray knew of their journey. She was getting fed up with all these people talking in riddles. "I'm not hungry. I just want to go home."

"Me too," Lynette said, putting down her spoon.

Edward nodded and also laid down his spoon.

Lucy glanced at Ewen and then at Mrs Murray. "Come,"

she said to the other three. "I think it's time you got some answers."

Caitlin scooped up Jack and she and Lynette and Edward followed Ewen and Lucy out of the kitchen.

Clan chief, Cameron of Locheil was sitting in a chair by the window in his temporary bedroom, his feet resting on a footstool. Both his ankles were wrapped in thick bandages.

He looked pale and tired, but he smiled as Mrs Murray showed them in. Lucy and Ewen went and perched on their father's bed. The three friends stood in a row, awkward and unsure.

"Don't look so scared," Mr Cameron said. "Come in. Come and sit." He pointed to a big sofa close to where he sat.

Lynette seemed to be the most alert and shoved the other two in the direction of the sofa. "Thanks, Mr Cameron," she said.

Mr Cameron smiled again. " Please, call me Locheil. That's what all my friends call me. You are most welcome here. And you," he said, looking at Caitlin. "You must be the Cameron girl."

Caitlin nodded. "How did you know?"

"Oh, I know my own," he said. "And there's the hair." He pointed at his own head and then Caitlin's. He too was a redhead. "From what I hear you're a brave one and worthy of the Cameron name." He turned to Edward. "And this must be the Farquharson boy."

"Yes, I'm Edward Farquharson. Pleased to meet you, sir."

"Ah, Edward, keeper of riches."

Edward looked puzzled and Ewen's father said, "Your name—Edward—it means keeper of riches. A fine name and a fine role. And the Farquharsons are also fine men. They fought and died well at the moor. You lost many kinsmen, as did the Camerons."

Then Locheil looked at Lynette. "And you must be Miss Maclean, Lynette, a name meaning leader. And I can see that it suits you."

Lynette beamed. "And what does Caitlin's name mean?" she asked.

"Ah, Caitlin—Caitlin means pure." Locheil looked serious now. He turned to Caitlin. "An appropriate name for someone with your role, I believe."

Now it was Caitlin's turn to look puzzled. Once again she felt impatient with all the mystery.

As if he read her thoughts, Ewen's father added, "And, I think it's high time your role and purpose in coming here were revealed to you."

"At last," Lynette said.

"Yes," Caitlin said. "What *are* we doing here?"

"You, Caitlin, are here because of your connections, your *family* connections. You are a direct descendant of one of Scottish history's most important women—"

"Flora Macdonald!" Caitlin said, remembering what her granny had said about the locket.

"Yes indeed!" Locheil said. "You know of her, that's good. Did you know that you are also related to Angus Chisholm, the young man you saved?"

Caitlin took a moment to take this in. "Oh," was all she could manage to say. It wasn't that she didn't have lots of questions. It was more that she didn't know where to start. "I know that Chisholm is my grandfather's name, and of course it was my mum's name too but..."

"I can see you are puzzled," Locheil said. "Don't worry, things will all fall into place. For now just try to see that life is full of threads and connections and that these links we share across time and space, they are meaningful. And, as I said, we too are related, Caitlin. You are a direct descendant of mine on your father's side of your family, and therefore you have another strong unbroken connection to this time and its events. Only ten generations separate you and me."

"Right, but you must have other descendants, and so

must this Flora woman. Why is it me who's here?" Caitlin asked.

"You're the third child of a third child, born in a palindromic year, close to the start of a new millennium, an auspicious time."

Caitlin nodded thoughtfully. "Right, so you're my great, great plus eight, or something, grandfather? And my mum and me were the third babies in our families. My birth year reads the same backwards as forwards. So what? It's just numbers."

"The numbers are important. Time, the universe, life itself, it's all about numbers. And all our days are indeed numbered. I have the honour to be a Time Keeper. And I must ensure the numbers remain as they should, that the lines and cogs of time flow smoothly in their interlocking circles and parallels, as the Universe intends."

"What?" Lynette said. "You mean everything's planned out. Nothing can happen by chance. We don't have any choice?"

"We all have choices," Locheil said. "And there is always an element of chance in everyone's lives. But alongside that, it's also true that history needs to play out in certain ways in order to bring our world to and through certain important junctions. Some things are too important or too terrible or too wonderful to simply be left completely to chance.

"I still really don't understand," Caitlin said. "You're a what, a Time Keeper? What does that mean? What does it have to do with me, with us?"

"I think he means you're special in some way," Edward said. "You and he are linked. He makes sure that time runs smoothly and that big events happen as and when they should. But something's gone wrong, and you're needed to put it right because you keep things pure, like your name says."

Ewen's father laughed. "Spot on, laddie! You're here to

support Caitlin. She's a Time Changer and you will guide and protect her on her mission."

Edward sat up straight, smiling. Caitlin looked at him. He seemed braver, stronger and, yes, happier than usual. She also glanced at Ewen. He didn't look happy. Then she realised what Locheil had just said.

"Sorry," Caitlin said. "I'm a what?"

"A Time Changer," Locheil replied. "You have the power to change events and therefore to change how time spins out through the ages."

"Oh," Caitlin said, not sure that she was any the wiser.

"What is it Caitlin has to do exactly?" Lynette asked. "We know from Lucy that it's something to do with Bonnie Prince Charlie."

Lucy gave a little gasp and looked at her father. "Sorry, I couldn't—"

"It's all right," her father said, raising a hand to quiet her. He turned to Lynette. "And you, Lynette the leader, you're right to be keen to move things along. Yes, Caitlin's task involves the Prince. With your help, she has to convince him of the course of action he must now follow."

Lynette looked pleased to be confirmed as right, and she asked, "And when Caitlin's done whatever it is she has to do for the Prince, we can go home?"

"Ah, well," Locheil leaned forward and looked at the three of them in turn, "The fact is you must all go home before she carries out her mission. And then you must return to see it through."

"What?" Caitlin said.

"Why?" Lynette said.

"How?" Edward said.

The three of them spoke all at once. But it was Ewen's voice that rose above the rest as he got to his feet. "Father," he said. "Father, let me do whatever it is. I can be a brave leader. I can put things right."

"Quiet, all of you!" Locheil raised his hands in the same gesture he'd used to silence Lucy.

"Son, I don't doubt your bravery or your ability to lead. And I admire your willingness to help. And you will get the chance to exercise all of these things. But you will do so in the here and now only. Now, sit, and I will explain."

Ewen sat down again beside Lucy. She put her hand on her brother's arm, but he shook her off. Caitlin felt sorry for him. She would gladly hand it all over to him, whatever *it* was. She tried to catch his eye, to smile at him, to let him know she understood how he felt. But he wouldn't look at her. She turned back to his father.

And, as the clock on the mantelpiece ticked the morning away, Cameron of Locheil, clan chief and a Time Keeper, told his descendant, Caitlin, a Time Changer, what it was she must do.

He told her she must return to 2014 and find proof that Bonnie Prince Charlie was saved from the Redcoats by a woman named Flora Macdonald. And he said that delivering this proof was in the best interests of Scotland. Proof was needed too, that even although the Prince's cause was lost, it was how it was meant to be. He said that both the Prince and this woman had other ideas about how history should play out. The Prince wanted to raise another army and to continue his fight to be king. And as for Flora Macdonald, she wasn't at all keen to give the Prince shelter at her island home. She was sure they would be caught and that she would be killed by the Redcoats. Both of them were wrong. Time and destiny would be hugely disrupted if they got their way.

"So, young Miss Cameron, do you think you can do it, go back to your own time, find the proof of the Prince's destiny and return here to deliver it to him?"

Caitlin wasn't at all sure about any of it. She could only nod, hesitantly.

"That's all very well," Edward said. "And I understand

what you say about the need to convince the Prince, but *how* do we prove to him that we're right?"

"Ah, young Edward," Locheil smiled as he spoke, "you're indeed a great thinker and already planning ahead. The proof will have to be some form of written documentation, perhaps also an artefact, a token that proves to both that all ends well. You'll need something that shows what the prince did in giving up the fight worked. He's a vain man. He'll want to see that he's remembered favourably and as some kind of hero."

"And when we've done all that, we can go home to the twenty-first century and stay there and go back to a normal life?" Lynette asked.

"When the mission is complete, you can indeed go home. As to whether life will remain *normal*, as you put it, who can tell?" Locheil shrugged.

"Do you mean I might have to do this sort of thing again?" Caitlin asked.

"You might be asked to, and you might not. Time Changers, Time Keepers, Seers—like you and me and Lucy—are spread throughout time and throughout the world. We all have specific roles to play although some of us will never be called on. Others, well, others of us can be asked to accomplish a lot. For some it will be some minor alteration, a tweak to the flow of time, and for others their tasks will be demanding and momentous."

"But if you're a Time Keeper," Lynette said, "Can you not travel into the twenty-first century and get the evidence you need? And why does it have to be the twenty-first century? Why not the nineteenth or twentieth centuries?"

"Good questions," Locheil said. "Firstly, Time Keepers cannot travel through time. Only Time Changers can do that. Time Keepers rely on Seers and on others, with greater knowledge, to keep an eye on how past and present will impact on the future. We are simply administrators and organisers. It is only the Time Changers who can move through time and go beyond their own lifetimes. And, as to why the twenty-first century, well, that's a lot to do with numbers, as I said before. Caitlin is the first Time Changer to come along since 1746 who has strong enough connections and, it has to be said, the right qualities. She is a descendant through all four of her grandparents of all the main people in these events. She is simply the best candidate. It's also the case that Scotland's history is once again at a turning point in the early twenty-first century, and it will be vital to prove to the Prince that his actions now, will be crucial for how things turn out.

"One thing I still don't understand is why Lynette and I ended up coming with Caitlin," Edward said. We're not special. We're not Time Changers or anything, are we?"

Locheil shrugged. "I can only guess that someone, perhaps another Time Keeper, one from your own time, deemed it appropriate that you and Lynette accompany Caitlin. After all, Lynette has proved her leadership qualities and you, you seem to be a perfect protector for Caitlin. Besides, three is a powerful number in our lives. The three fates; the Christian belief in Father, Son and Holy Ghost; the body, mind and soul."

"The three bears," Lynette said.

"The three little pigs," Caitlin said and she and Lynette both giggled, but it was a nervous and tense sort of a giggle.

"The three musketeers," Edward said, more seriously.

Locheil frowned. "Past, present and future, the eternal triangle," he said. "And you three, you are the three sides of a triangle of friendship, strong and interconnected. I've no doubt you all have your part to play."

"So," Lynette said, her giggles all gone. "We go back, get this proof and return here with it. Then the Prince and this Flora woman do what they're supposed to do for the good of Scotland and we go home once more, job done."

"Yes, that's it."

"And can I ask why you?" Edward said. "Why is it *you* that we've been brought to?"

"Another excellent observation, young man," Locheil said. "As I said I'm a Time Keeper, and yes there are other Keepers, but I'm also a close associate of the Prince. We are friends and he trusts me. I can make sure you get access to him when the time comes."

"So how do we get back, back home I mean, and then how do we return here, when we've got what you need?" Caitlin asked.

"You'll be shown to a portal. A jumping off point. It will be similar to how you got here in the first place. And, when you've got what you need, you'll be guided back."

"Who? Who will guide us to the portal for coming back?" Edward asked.

"There will be someone, there must be someone in your time, who knows of Caitlin's role. I'm certain whoever it is will make themselves known to you, if they haven't already done so?" Locheil looked at Caitlin.

Caitlin's hand went to her pocket and to Bella's note. She looked at Edward and Lynette. "Bella," the three of them said together.

Caitlin nodded. "I think we know who it is. But I wonder why she didn't say something before all this happened. Then we could have been prepared."

"Hmm, yes, I admit it's strange you had no warning. That I can't explain."

"So, when will we go to this—this portal?" Lynette asked.

"Very soon," Locheil replied. "Before this day is out. Lucy has seen where it is and Ewen will escort you."

Ewen immediately jumped up. "Yes, yes I will," he said.

His father smiled at him. Then he looked back at the other three, his expression serious once more. "But on your return you must find your own way back to us from the portal , back to us here at Achnaharrie. You'll have to do that without our help as we have no way of knowing the exact moment when you'll return."

"How long have we got to get the proof back here?" Edward asked.

"Ah, now that's a good question," Locheil replied. "The simplest answer I can give is, it will take as long as it takes. It's true that time waits for no man. But in the case of a Time Changer's work, as long as she or he is acting in good faith and for the greater good, then time will pace itself to the action."

Edward frowned with concentration. "So, are you saying we'll get the time we need as long as we don't waste any?"

"Yes, exactly so."

"But, hang on?" Lynette said, looking very confused. "Won't time be passing here? Won't things be happening? The Prince doing what he wants to do and this Flora woman refusing to help? We could be too late."

"Yes, you could. But, during periods of Timechanging activities, time can be slowed or even paused if necessary on either side of a portal, but not indefinitely. It's important to be aware of that. There will be a build-up of time pressure. The size of any time lag will gradually lengthen. Any time wasted by the Time Changer during a mission such as yours will add to the pressure."

"So the quicker we are the better?" Edward asked. "If we take too long, or if we fail, then the flow of time will equalise again and events here will start to move along?"

"Precisely," Locheil replied. "But, as I've said, if you put in maximum effort and make optimum progress, then only when you return here will time's normal passage resume. And when your mission is complete and you've gone home, time will stabilise on both sides."

"And this time pause thing," Caitlin said, "is it the case that at home, our home in the twenty-first century, time is moving much more slowly than it is here, now?"

"It could be. If necessary," Locheil said.

Caitlin nodded, beginning to get her head round it. If time had been moving much more slowly at home then it could be they'd only been gone an hour or two and had indeed not been missed.

"All very neat," Lynette said. "But if a Time Changer fails, what then?"

"Then time is disrupted and all sorts of evil can and does break through. Events move on and the course of time is changed. It has happened throughout history. Sometimes a Time Changer's task has been too much for them and all hell has broken loose..." Locheil paused and looked around at them all, at their now very serious faces.

He smiled kindly. "Fear not," he said. "From what I've seen of you three young people from the future, and from what I know of my own two brave and strong children, I have no doubt you will succeed."

Locheil held his out his arms to Ewen and Lucy who went to him. He hugged them both. "Now go, all of you. Lucy, you know your part. Ewen take good care of our visitors and follow where you sister leads." He turned then to Caitlin, Lynette and Edward. "Godspeed to all of you. I will see you upon your return, whenever that may be."

Chapter Seventeen

Caitlin, Edward and even Lynette wanted to say goodbye to Hero before they set off for the portal and home so Ewen took them round to the stables.

"Don't worry," Ewen said, as Caitlin patted Hero's head and the horse nuzzled her hand. "Father says Hero can stay here until you return."

Caitlin nodded. Hero meant so much to her already that she didn't think she could speak without crying. It was going to be difficult to leave him behind. Lynette squeezed her arm. Caitlin could see that her friend knew how she was feeling. She moved away from Hero. Edward then said his goodbyes. He seemed to be saying something to the horse but Caitlin couldn't make out what it was. Hero snorted and whinnied.

"We better go," Lucy said. "Father said the timing is important. We need to be at the portal very soon."

And so the group set off. Ewen and Lucy leading, and the other three following. Caitlin had Jack on the lead. Now would not be a good time for him to go running off. Ewen had the key for the padlocked gates and they all slipped out of Achnaharrie's grounds unnoticed.

They walked along the road, keeping close to the hedgerows in case they needed a hiding place. They headed back in the direction they had come the day before. Caitlin noticed that Edward was writing in his notebook as they walked.

After about a mile, Lucy led them off the road and into a

wooded area. They stopped beside a tall Scots pine. Lucy put her hand on it. It was just like the pine tree at the Hermitage, it had several trunks and its bark was gnarled and knotted with age. It was another granny pine. Caitlin noticed how quiet the wood had become. There was no birdsong, no scuffling of birds or animals, not even a rustle from the leaves of the other trees. It was if the wood was holding its breath. Lucy frowned and put her hand to her forehead as if she was in pain. She let out a little moan.

"Are you all right?" Ewen asked, looking at his sister.

She nodded. "Yes, yes, I'm fine. Father says it's because I'm not used to the power of the visions. It won't always be like this."

"So, is this the place?" Edward asked. "Is this where we leave from?"

"Yes," Lucy replied. "This is it. You arrived at the base of a Scots pine tree on the edge of Culloden Moor, didn't you?"

Lynette and Caitlin exchanged a look, eyebrows raised.

"I saw you," Lucy said. "I was thinking about Father and Ewen, wondering if they were all right, wondering how it was with the Redcoats on the battlefield and I saw you – all three of you and the dog as you arrived. It was like you just slid out of the tree."

"We were leaning against a pine tree when we left 2014," Edward said. "So is that how it works? We travel by tree?"

Lucy smiled. "Sort of. I think so. The Granny pines act as portals, as gateways through time. At the right point in time, and with the right people assembled, all you have to do is touch the trunk and the portal opens."

Edward frowned as he thought about this and then he said, "So you go through the portal and you fall through time, like you're on a giant flume or in a rabbit hole, and then you land beside another pine tree somewhere else, and in another time?"

"I don't know what a flume is, but yes, a rabbit hole is

probably a good description," Lucy said.

"And the tree knows where to send you?" Lynette asked. "I mean we could have ended up anywhere, anytime when we came here but the tree knew 1746 at Culloden."

"Yes, it would seem the trees do know," Lucy said. "Some live for hundreds of years and they whisper to each other, tree to tree, forest to forest and year to year." She put her hand on the pine tree's bark again. "It's time," she said.

"What do we do?" Caitlin asked.

Lynette stepped forward. "Like Ed said, when we came here from the Hermitage, we were all leaning on the tree. Remember?"

"Makes sense," Caitlin said. "We better say goodbye." She looked at Ewen. "Thank you for bringing us to your father. We could have been stranded forever if you hadn't found us."

"It seems like it was meant to be," Ewen said, smiling.

"Goodbye, both of you," Caitlin said.

"We'll see you when you return," Lucy said.

Ewen stepped forward. "For you," he said, looking at Edward. He held out a strip of tartan, Cameron tartan, and he reached round and tied it to the end of the mapstick which still poked out of the top of Edward's bag.

"Thanks," Edward said and he and Ewen shook hands.

Caitlin tucked Jack under her arm, then she and Edward and Lynette stood by the tree, their backs against one of its trunks.

"Goodbye!" they called.

"Goodbye!" Ewen and Lucy shouted, as the wind picked up and the birds began to sing again.

Then the falling began.

Caitlin felt a shudder run through her body. It was like you sometimes experience as you're going to sleep, and you feel like you're falling, and your body does a strange jumpy thing. She opened her eyes.

She was back in the Hermitage, sitting at the foot of

the pine tree, overlooking the bike racks. Her book and her backpack were in her lap, along with Jack. Edward was beside her, his bag on his shoulder. Lynette was on Caitlin's other side, her legs stretched out in front of her and her feet in third position.

The three friends looked at each other.

"What just happened?" Lynette asked. "Was I asleep?"

"I don't know, but I was definitely asleep," Edward said. "And I had such a weird dream."

"Me too," Lynette said.

"No, I don't think either of you've been asleep or dreaming," Caitlin said. "Look at your mapstick, Ed. Where did that come from?"

The other two looked at where Caitlin was pointing. A piece of Cameron tartan fluttered on the end alongside the original Stuart strip that had been there before.

The three of them looked at each other in silence. Each of them trying to make sense of recent events. Each of them wondering if the others had experienced the same thing.

"According to this," Edward said, pointing at his watch, "It's five to four in the afternoon on August the 12th, 2014, which is close to what it said before we—before we—"

"So, it's working again, is it?" Lynette asked.

"Yes, the second hand's moving," Edward said. "So, you knew it had stopped? I didn't just dream that?"

"Yes, we knew," Caitlin said. "We both knew. Mine stopped too while we were there in 1746 with—"

"Okay," Lynette said, raising her hands. "Okay, this is freaking me out. Are we saying that none of us has been dreaming. Are we saying that we've all been away, all of us, together, away to another time and place for three days, and now we're back. And while we were away, time here, in 2014, just about stood still?"

"Yes, remember what Ewen's father said about time," Caitlin said.

"Ewen!" Lynette said. "Ewen?" she looked at Edward.

Edward nodded. "Yes, Ewen," he said. "We were all there. We all met Ewen. He gave me the tartan for the mapstick. It all really happened."

The three friends sat with their backs against the pine tree and spent the next little while going over the adventure they'd just had, trying to make sense of it all. Watching for bike thieves was the last thing on their minds.

They all jumped when Caitlin's mobile phone beeped in her bag. She scrambled to get it out. The low-power warning was flashing but there was also a text from Bella.

Hope you are ok. You must be tired. Come home soon. B x

"Bella's got something to do with it, with what happened today, hasn't she?" Lynette said.

"Yes, definitely." Caitlin stood up. "And we should go home right now and ask her about it."

The other two stood up as well. They collected Edward's father's bike, the only one at the bike rack, and set off for Caitlin's house.

Chapter Eighteen

"Welcome back," Bella said as the three friends and Jack walked into the kitchen. Jack was very excited to see Bella and jumped and yelped with joy. As she patted Jack and got him to calm down, Bella smiled at them all. "You've had quite an adventure," she said.

On the table were plates of sandwiches, a bowl of crisps, and a jug of juice. There was also a large sponge cake covered with yellow icing. Bella pointed at the food. "I thought you might be hungry."

"Oh, yes!" Edward said. He walked past Bella and sat down at the table. "I'm Edward, by the way," he added.

Bella looked at him and laughed. "I thought you probably were. I'm very pleased to meet you." She turned to Lynette and held out her hand. "And you must be Lynette. I'm Bella."

"Pleased to meet you," Lynette said as they shook hands. Lynette stared at Bella as if she couldn't quite believe what she was seeing.

But Bella didn't notice Lynette's stare as she was looking at Caitlin, looking at her puzzled, tired face. "Caitlin, my dear child, are you okay?"

Caitlin nodded. "Yes, yes I'm okay."

"But you have lots of questions?" Bella asked.

Caitlin nodded again. She bit her lip. She wasn't sure which of all the feelings she was experiencing was the strongest. She felt bewildered, even a bit cross, but she also felt very happy and relieved to be home, and excited and tired as well.

"I know it's a lot to take in," Bella said. "I know you're bound to be feeling quite mixed up after everything that happened. Come and sit down. You too, Lynette. All of you, tuck in and I'll do my best to explain."

Once the children were all seated at the table and enjoying the most wonderful afternoon tea, Bella began. "I know you've been much further away than the Hermitage this afternoon. You travelled far away and far back in time. All the way to Culloden in 1746."

"I found your note," Caitlin said. "So we know that you knew what was happening to us, and we've guessed from what we were told by a man called Cameron of Locheil that you are a Time Keeper. Is that right?"

"Yes, yes it is," Bella said. "I am indeed a Time Keeper. And I hoped the note would offer you some reassurance, but also that it wouldn't confuse you with too much information."

"I don't think we could have got any more confused," Lynette said.

"Why didn't you warn us, warn me?" Caitlin frowned at Bella. "It would have been much less confusing if you'd explained beforehand."

"Ah, well, yes, I know I should have warned you, and I was going to. But events rather overtook us, I'm afraid."

"How did they?"

"Angus—Angus Chisholm? The boy you saved—"

"Yes, what about him? What about Angus?" Caitlin said.

"It was a last minute thing apparently. He ran away to fight, to fight at Culloden. His father had warned him not to, that he was too young, but he went anyway and it wasn't meant to happen. Then he got seriously injured. There was nothing in the time-plan to foretell it and nothing in place to save him. So you had to go early."

"Why me? And how do you know it wasn't meant to happen? Maybe…" Caitlin hesitated It was a horrible and upsetting thought, but… "Maybe he was meant to be killed."

Bella shook her head. "No, no he wasn't. If he'd died, then you and your brother and sister, you wouldn't exist. You wouldn't have been born, and neither would your mother or grandfather or anyone in that line of your family, going all the way back to—"

"Angus," Caitlin said.

"Yes, he's in direct line to you. And if he'd died, then…" Bella raised her eyebrows and shook her head.

"Then I wouldn't be here now." Caitlin took a minute to take this in.

"And since you were going anyway, to that time and place, it made sense just to send you and not involve another Time Changer. Besides, the original plan was that you'd meet up with Ewen Cameron and his father at their home—because of Locheil's connections to the Prince—and events would proceed from there. It just meant you met with Ewen a bit earlier and then had to find Locheil."

"You make it sound so simple," Lynette said. "But what if we hadn't met up with Ewen on the battlefield? What if we hadn't passed by the place where Angus was?"

"I know it wasn't simple and I know it must have been very frightening to be at the battlefield. But it was carefully worked out that you'd emerge beside Ewen and that your route off the field would take you past Angus," said Bella.

"So when did you first know about Angus?"

"Only yesterday, I saw something in this." Bella produced her snowstorm ornament from her bag. "I saw Angus lying wounded on the battlefield. And I saw you, or rather your birth certificate. It was fading. I consulted my—my advisor— and she told me I had to get you back to 1746 a bit earlier than planned. "

"Did you know that the Hermitage was where we'd have to leave from? Did you know about the trees?" asked Caitlin.

"Yes, again, I saw it in here." Bella pointed to the snowstorm. "I saw the sign that stands at the Hermitage entrance and I know that trees are one of the commonest access points to the time portals. I was advised that the Hermitage was a place you liked to visit, but I needed a way to make sure you and your friends would return there today and be in the proximity of the right pine tree. So I—"

"It was you!" Lynette said. "You stole our bikes so we'd have a reason to go back."

Bella looked a bit embarrassed. "Well, yes. I didn't actually steal them myself, but I did arrange it. Sorry. But you mustn't worry. The police will shortly receive a tip-off about where to find them and they will be returned to you."

"But how did you know we'd go back and stakeout the bike racks?" Edward asked.

"I couldn't be sure, of course. I was actually working on my own plan for ensuring you'd go back, but when Caitlin told me you were all going back anyway, all I had to do was offer encouragement and support."

"Wasn't it a bit irresponsible?" Caitlin said. "Most adults probably wouldn't recommend that children go looking for criminals."

Again Bella looked a bit embarrassed. "Yes, I know, you're right. But it seemed the quickest and easiest way of ensuring you'd be close to the portal at the right time. Besides, there were no real thieves and I knew Jack would be with you. *And* I followed you, to make sure you were all right."

"I knew it!" Caitlin said. "I knew someone was watching. Were you there yesterday too, when we were at the edge of the burn and we saw the heron?"

"Yes, yes I was. I had to make sure you were well away from the bike racks while your bikes were being dealt with."

For a little while the children were quiet. They ate the sandwiches and the cake, which was delicious, and drank the ice-cold apple juice. And they thought about what Bella had told them so far.

It was Caitlin who broke the silence. "I get what you say about Angus," she said looking at Bella. "And I understand about it all being a rush, but couldn't you have tried to explain it to me last night?"

"I did consider it, but I knew I wouldn't get enough time alone with you. I also suspected it would simply be too much for you to make sense of in the time available. I did try to indicate a bit about the possibilities of time travel when we were talking with Fiona but I couldn't take it too far. In the end, I really thought it best that you and your friends just go and get on with it."

"That's another thing," Lynette said. "Why did you involve Ed and me? After all we might have been no help to Caitlin at all."

Bella smiled. "I never doubted that you and Edward were absolutely necessary and perfectly suitable as companions and helpers for Caitlin. I've been watching all three of you for some time now. In here." She put her hand on the snowstorm. "I've been getting to know you all ever since I was made aware of the likelihood of this mission, and the identity of the Time Changer."

"Oh," Lynette said, sounding surprised.

"The loyalty you have to one another, the strength of your friendship and your self-reliance and courage were all obvious to me," said Bella.

"Courage?" Edward said. "I'm not brave."

Bella smiled at him. "Edward you are very brave. You did some very courageous things while you were away."

"Yes he did," Caitlin said. "But how do you know?"

"Oh, I was keeping a very close eye on you. I had the birds, and Jack, of course, and all manner of people and things helping me do so," Bella said.

"The birds?" Caitlin said.

"Jack?" Lynette said.

"What people and things?" Edward said.

Bella took a deep breath. "Birds are marvellous messengers. Do you remember, Caitlin? We spoke about them."

Caitlin nodded.

"Some birds are capable of navigating and flying over huge distances," Bella continued. "Swallows, for example, fly to this country from Africa. They eat and sleep on the wing and they don't get lost. But even the birds who don't migrate, they spend a lot of time flying. Nobody really knows where they go. We know where they feed and where they nest and roost. But what about their time in the air?"

The children just looked at Bella. "What about it?" Lynette said.

"They travel. And not just over distances through space, but some travel across time too. They're not bound by the same dimensions and constraints as we are. They can flit from timeline to timeline, from the cogs of the present to those of the past and future."

"Even if that's true," Caitlin said, unsure whether to believe it or not, "how did it help us, or help you to help us?"

"Messages!" Edward said. "The birds carried messages between Bella and somebody who was with us in 1746. That's right, isn't it?"

Bella smiled at Edward. "Indeed it is! You met Mrs Baxter, the cook at Fraser's place. And then there was Izzie at Angus's home and Mrs Murray at the Cameron place. All three are ancestors of mine, from different branches of the family, and all three were Seers like Lucy. I was able to write notes to them, and I entrusted these notes to various members of the group of birds who visit the garden here. And those three ladies wrote back to me about who you were with, what you were doing and to reassure me that all was well with you."

"Your ring!" Caitlin said, remembering. "Mrs Baxter—she has—had one just like it."

Bella smiled. She looked down at the ring on her finger.

"One and the same," she said. "Passed down through the family to me."

Again the children took a moment to get their heads round it all, not least the fact of all those birds flying through time. Then Lynette said, "You mentioned that Jack helped you keep an eye on us. How did that work?"

"Ah, Jack Russell," Bella said. She reached down to where he was snoozing at her feet and she picked the dog up and sat with him in her lap, stroking his head and scratching behind his ears as she talked. "My brave wee Jack," she said. "Jack is able to use rabbit holes as roads to other times. He was able to travel easily and freely between now and 1746, although not as rapidly as the birds could travel through the air. As you can imagine some of the notes I needed to send, especially at first, they were quite lengthy, full of explanation, and therefore too big to attach to the rather delicate leg of a garden bird. So he was invaluable as the bearer of these longer and very important messages. He was also able to reassure me that you were all okay."

"How did he do that?" Caitlin asked.

"I expect it was much like Hero, and how he communicated with me," Edward said.

Bella smiled at Edward again. "You have an amazingly quick mind, Edward," she said. "All that time you spend not talking, but just observing, you put it to very good use. And you're right. As with yourself and Hero, Jack and I can communicate without words."

"I haven't managed to figure it all out," Edward said. "For example, is there someone in charge of it all, in charge of all of time?"

"I can't tell you every detail. That's not allowed. It's need to know only. But I do have a boss, an Eternal Invigilator, a person whose job it is to keep watch and alert the appropriate Time Keepers when there is a job to be done. It was my boss who sent me the message about Caitlin and who organised it so that the childcare agency would send me to look after her."

"An Eternal Invigilator?" Edward said. "Who's that? What do they do? Do they live forever?"

"I don't know their identity. Time Keepers never meet their Invigilator. And no they don't live forever. None of us do. Every generation has its own individuals, its own Keepers, Changers and Seers, chosen by the Invigilators. No one person can do more than one of those jobs, that way no single person can have too much power."

"And who chooses the Invigilators?" Lynette asked.

"Another good question!" Bella said. "The existing Invigilators are always on the lookout for likely candidates amongst the Keepers, Changers and Seers. Any of them can propose a candidate and they'll all vote on whether to offer the post of Invigilator to the individual in question."

"Sounds fair," Lynette said. "And what exactly do the Invigilators do?"

"Invigilators keep a close eye on the timelines," Bella answered. "They look for anomalies, and decide if action has to be taken. They will decide the most appropriate Time Keepers, Changers and Seers for any missions, and the relevant Invigilator will alert the chosen Time Keeper to organise it all. All communication is done quietly and on a need-to-know basis."

"And how do they keep watch exactly? How do they communicate?" Caitlin asked.

"At this point in time, it's all done by computers. PCs, laptops, tablets and of course satellite links. It used to be that Invigilators and Time Keepers could only tap into the web of knowledge by scroll, book or by crystal ball, or by the interpretation of the stars and the signs in nature. Communication would be by messenger. And today some still favour these more traditional methods. I must say I'm still a great believer in using my snowstorms, and I know you've noticed my Time Keeper's clock on my bag, Caitlin."

"Yes, yes I have," Caitlin said. "I didn't think it was an ordinary sewn-on picture."

"Indeed it is not," Bella replied. "It's activated when a Time Changer's mission is activated. Gives a second by second countdown. It has never let me down. But I must admit that there are some amazing apps for Time Keepers nowadays, and being able to email and text message has meant that we can react very quickly when time anomalies occur."

"Apps – for Keepers of time?" Lynette said. "That sounds cool. Can you get them at the app store?"

Bella laughed. "I can. But they're only available to people like me. They and the relevant websites are password protected."

"Right," Lynette said.

"When did you first know that you were a Time Keeper? Was it while you were still a child?" Caitlin asked.

Bella shook her head. "It was when I was a teenager that I first became aware that I was different. I started having these visions, seeing things that were happening in other times and places. I was so scared by them, I told my mother. She wasn't surprised. As it turned out she too was a Seer and her mother, my grandmother, had been a Time Keeper. Not only that, my aunt had been a Time Changer in her youth. And then, when I was much older, I was appointed as a Keeper and my abilities as a Seer faded. All this stuff tends to run in families."

"It does?" Caitlin said. "Is anyone else in my family like me? Can anyone else travel in time?"

"Your grandmother in Skye, she's a Seer, and so was your mother. In fact I worked with your mother. An event involving William Wallace. She had excellent abilities. I'm sure she'd have been made a Time Keeper had she lived, maybe even an Invigilator. She was very talented."

"Oh," Caitlin said, swallowing hard. Bella reached over and patted her hand. Caitlin looked at Bella. "You knew my mum?"

"I did. It was a long time ago, before you were born. She was a lovely lady. So it was particularly pleasing when I was alerted to your existence and to your role, and to the fact that I'd be working with you."

"How come Caitlin's granny didn't tell her about all of this?" Lynette asked. "My gran can never keep a secret about anything and she's always banging on about family history and stuff."

"Ah," Bella said, "we, that is those of us involved in the watching, keeping and fixing of time, we aren't permitted to discuss our work with anyone who doesn't possess our powers and abilities, no matter how close they may be to us. Our powers are awesome and must be guarded and protected from interference or abuse."

"But Lynette and I have no special powers," Edward said. "And yet we've been told and we've been involved in helping."

"Yes, that's true," Bella replied. "Occasionally, ordinary people, that is people only concerned with the here-and-now, are given Need-to-Know status in order to support a Time Changer or Keeper."

"And afterwards, what happens? Are our memories wiped or something?" Edward asked.

Bella smiled. "No, nothing like that. You are simply asked not to discuss or share anything related to these—these special events—with anyone other than Seers, Time Keepers, Time Changers and other Need-to-Knows."

"Um," Lynette said, looking worried. "We told Angus and of course Ewen knows."

"It's all right," Bella said. "Both of them are Need-to-Knows."

"Right," Lynette said. "And if we did tell someone we shouldn't then..."

"Who knows?" Bella said. "There are no sanctions as such. Whenever someone has said something they shouldn't, and it does happen, then the least harmful outcome has been that they haven't been believed, and the worst outcome has meant that a mission has not been fulfilled and all hell has broken loose. We therefore ask that you don't tell those who don't need to know."

"Okay," Edward said. "So we know the rules, we know the mission and we know we need documents and maybe an object that will make Bonnie Prince Charlie see he can and should escape to France. We have to have something that will make him believe he's remembered as a Scottish hero. We also need to convince Flora Macdonald she's meant to help him."

"Absolutely correct," Bella said with a grin on her face.

"But how exactly are we supposed to do that?" Edward asked. "And what documents? What objects?"

"There are lots of historical records of what happened after 1746. There are the history books, there are copies of several relevant documents online, there are paintings, songs, poems..." Bella smiled at them. "Don't worry, with you three great minds working together, I'm sure you'll do just fine."

Bella stopped and looked round at the children's serious faces. "I think that's probably enough questions and answers for now. You've been through a lot. I suggest that if you've all had enough to eat then you two, Edward and Lynette, go home and get some rest. As for you, Caitlin, I suggest you go and have a nice hot bath and give me these muddy clothes of yours so I can get them washed.

Chapter Nineteen

Caitlin didn't really understand what 'all hell breaking loose' would be like. As well as Bella saying it, she remembered it was also an expression Locheil had used. However, after her trip to 1746 she thought she knew what being hit by a tornado might feel like. The remaining few days of the summer holidays passed in an absolute whirl. Caitlin felt as if she'd never talked or thought or questioned so much in her life. She talked a lot with Bella and Edward and Lynette. Bella reassured them that they weren't wasting time in any way that would affect their mission and that a bit of a pause was necessary for their preparations. She encouraged them just to enjoy what was left of the holidays and to have lots of fun.

Caitlin found she trusted Bella more and more, and not only as a Time Keeper, but as her childminder. Her dad seemed to feel the same as far as Bella's qualities as a nanny were concerned, because he asked Bella to stay on as a permanent replacement for Susie. Caitlin had to admit to herself that she was very pleased when Bella accepted.

Caitlin's dad was working extra-long hours. And although Caitlin didn't like that she hardly saw him, it did lessen the danger of her letting anything slip about what had happened. It was the same with Fiona and James who were also hardly at home. They always seemed to be out at their holiday jobs or away doing stuff with their friends. However, with Bella around she never felt lonely.

Bella's prediction about their bikes proved to be true and

they got them back the day after their return from 1746. The police said they'd had an anonymous phone call telling them where to find the bikes and it had proved to be correct. The police also said they still had no idea who had stolen the bikes in the first place.

In what felt like no time, it was the last Friday of the holidays. Edward, Lynette and Caitlin were in Caitlin's bedroom

Lynette sat crosslegged at the end of Caitlin's bed. "This has been one crazy week," she said.

"It sure has," Caitlin said. She was also sitting on the bed, but at the pillow end.

Edward, who'd been spinning slowly on the swivel chair at Caitlin's desk, stopped twirling round and said, "But at least we know now exactly what we've got to do and when we've got to do it by."

"Oh, yeah, no worries there," Lynette said. "We just have to find evidence of Flora Macdonald's important role in saving Bonnie Prince Charlie. Evidence that'll convince her to risk her life to save him and will convince her she'll be safe." She jumped down off the bed and began to do pas-de-chats steps around it. "And," she went on, as she danced, "we also have to find a way to make the Prince believe he must give up the fight and go to France, and that doing so would be best for Scotland. *And* we have to do it as soon as possible. Simple!"

"It shouldn't be that hard," Edward said. "There'll be the library at high school and we'll have a proper history teacher. Maybe he or she can help us."

Lynette looked sceptical. "Yeah right, we just go up to them and say, we realise you're probably just a plain old Here-and-Now type person, but we're special, and we need your help with a mission back in 1746."

"No. Don't be stupid. Of course not," Edward said. "I just meant we'd have access to lots more information and experts once we're at school."

"Don't call me stupid!" Lynette glowered at Edward.

"Well, you—"

"You two, please, don't fall out," Caitlin said. "I need you both, together and on my side. I can't do any of this time-changing stuff on my own. I need you two with me, my two best friends. Let's try to stay calm. Like Bella said, we should concentrate on settling into high school and then take it from there."

"Yeah, okay," Lynette said.

"Ed?" Caitlin said. "Look at me, Ed. You're with me, yeah?"

Edward looked at her. "Yes, of course I am. I just think Lynette is panicking and there's no need."

Lynette made a face and then flopped back down on the bed. "I don't see why Bella can't do it. She's a grown-up. She could go and find all the evidence and give it to us, or she could even take it herself. I mean she's the one who knows everything."

Caitlin shook her head. "No, she can't do it. That's not her role. Time Keepers don't time travel. It's only Time Changers, and their assistants of course, who can travel in time. And it's Time Changers who have to do the important work so that it comes from the heart."

"You know all this, Lynette," Edward said. "Bella explained it all to us."

"Yeah, I know, it's just—well—I can't really get my head round it, that's all," Lynette said. "I mean a week ago we were just ordinary kids, and now we've got missions and responsibility and it's—it's scary." Lynette bit her lip and looked as if she was going to cry.

"Oh, Lynnie," Caitlin said. She moved down the bed, put her arm round Lynette's shoulder. "Don't get upset. I know it's a lot to take in. I'm finding it hard myself. But you don't have to do this. Not if it's going to upset you."

Lynette rubbed at her tears with the back of her hand.

"No, no. I'm coming. There's no way I'd let you go without me."

"Thank goodness for that," Caitlin said, smiling and hugging her friend. "I need you *and* Ed. I need my two brave friends to help me."

Lynette gave a little smile and sniffed loudly.

Edward took a hankie out of his pocket, a real cotton hankie, not a paper one. He held it out to Lynette. "Here," he said. "You can wipe your tears with this."

Lynette took the hankie. "Thanks, Ed." She blew her nose and dried her tears. "You're the only person I know who uses real hankies."

"My mother always makes me have one in my pocket. She'll be pleased I've used one at long last."

"Hmm, but will she be pleased when she knows it was me who used it?" Lynette laughed.

Edward shrugged and smiled. "I'll just tell her it was me. She'll be very proud." He took the hankie back and stuffed it in his pocket. "You've done me a favour."

"I'm glad you two are friends again," Caitlin said.

"I'm sorry, sorry for being grumpy. I don't know what gets into me sometimes. Mum says it's hormones."

"Yeah, I know what you mean," Caitlin said. "I get like that too. Fiona says it's to do with—you know..." She glanced at Edward who'd gone back to twirling on the chair. "It's to do with girls' monthly cycles."

"Cycles?" Edward said. "What on earth have your bikes got to do with your bad moods? And anyway, you've got them back. That should make you happy!"

Caitlin and Lynette looked at each other and then they started laughing. They laughed until the tears ran down their faces. Ed just looked mystified.

"And you, Caitlin, how do you feel about it all?" Lynette asked, as they got over their giggles. "I mean it's been a shock for all three of us, but for you, well, you've got this special job and nobody asked you if you wanted it."

"I feel okay now. I didn't at first, but since Bella told me about my gran and my mum, it's kind of made it easier. You know? It feels right."

Lynette nodded. "What about you Ed? How do you feel? Are you really up for staying with Caitlin and seeing this thing through, even though it's all a bit weird and doesn't make any sense?"

"Of course I am," Edward said. "Things never make much sense to me at first. This time travel thing isn't any different. It's no more scary than anything else. I'm used to the world being weird."

Caitlin smiled and Lynette said, "Fair enough."

"So, we're agreed," Caitlin said.

"We could just look stuff up on the internet," Lynette said. "Wikipedia's probably got loads of stuff about Bonnie Prince Charlie."

"Yeah, but Fiona says you have to be careful with stuff on the internet. Not all of it is checked. We'd be better off looking for real books and stuff," Caitlin said. "Ed's idea about the school library and the history teacher is a good one."

"And, remember, you'll need proof about your family tree, you know, to prove to the Prince and Flora Macdonald who you are," Edward said.

"Yeah, well, I vote we take a break from 1746 for our last weekend of freedom," Lynette said. "Let's go out."

"Yes," Caitlin said. "Where will we go?"

"Anywhere except the Hermitage," Edward said.

Chapter Twenty

The first week at their new school was exhausting, exciting and very different to primary school. They'd been for induction visits, of course, but that wasn't quite like being there for real. Caitlin, Lynette and Edward were in the same register class and were in the same class for some subjects, but not for others. However, they met up every break and lunchtime.

Following a timetable and moving classrooms every forty-five minutes took a bit of getting used to, as did the sheer size of the building. And then there were all the extra pupils. There were so many new names to get to know, pupils and staff, and the fifth and sixth years looked like grown-ups.

However, Caitlin was pleasantly surprised how well Edward was coping with the move. He was talking to more people than he used to. He had actually been able to ask for help from adults in the school when he needed it. He had a lady like Mrs Maxwell that was with him in some of his classes, but he didn't always have an adult helper with him. There was also a special room for him, and any other pupils who found high school a bit difficult at times, to go to at break and lunchtime, and even for timeout during class time if they needed to, but so far Edward hadn't needed to. He sometimes even spoke to the teachers in his classes.

And of course there were Craig and Corinna to contend with. But they didn't seem to be bothering Caitlin, Lynette and Edward so much. They'd tried a bit in the first few days.

They'd met them in the corridor and in the playground, and they were in some of the same classes. Then, one lunchtime, Craig had stopped Edward and the girls in the canteen and asked Edward where his mapsticks were. Edward had astounded Caitlin and Lynette with his response. Craig and Corinna had been shocked too.

"Mapsticks?" Edward said. "They're for little kids. I don't do them anymore. I prefer drawing out memory maps. I would explain these to you, if I thought you were intelligent enough to understand, but you're not, so I won't. Now get out of my way. I want to eat my lunch." Then he'd pushed past Craig, shaken his head at Corinna , who'd been lurking behind Craig, and gone to join the lunch queue.

"My goodness!" Lynette said as she and Caitlin caught up with him. "You've changed! That was brave."

"Yeah, well done, Ed. Well done for sticking up for your-self," Caitlin said.

Edward just shrugged. "After all we saw and did in 1746, that was nothing."

After that, the worst thing Craig and Corinna did was to scowl at the three friends whenever they met, but otherwise they left them alone.

And it wasn't very long before Caitlin, Edward and Lynette felt like they'd always been at high school.

It was during the second week that Mr Carnie, their history teacher, made an exciting announcement. He told the class that they could choose what aspect of history they'd like to study for the next three weeks. He said they were to work in trios and that each trio had to submit their proposal within the week. Then, if he approved their submission, they would have three weeks to put together a file on their chosen topic. There would be a prize for the best one.

Mr Carnie got the class to brainstorm the sort of things they'd need to do for producing a topic file and they made a mind map of all the suggestions on the interactive whiteboard. Mr Carnie then printed and copied the mind map for everyone in the class and gave them a few minutes to sort themselves into trios. Caitlin, Lynette and Edward immediately went together. For the rest of the lesson Mr Carnie talked through some hints and tips about how to go about the project and gave the pupils details of what he'd be looking for.

When Caitlin and her two friends met up at lunchtime, there was only one topic of conversation.

"Well, the history project is perfect isn't it?" Lynette said.

"Yeah," Caitlin said, grinning. "Like it was meant to be."

"Written in the timeline most likely," Edward said. It was difficult to tell if he was joking, but then Edward rarely joked.

"Whatever, it's good news for us," Lynette said.

"So, we should get cracking on our proposal right away," Caitlin said. "Do you want to come over to mine tonight after dinner and we'll work on it together?"

The other two agreed.

That evening, when the three of them were settled at Caitlin's desk, Edward said, "I've had an idea. I think we should do the project as a 'What If'."

"Brilliant!" Lynette said. Then she added, "Eh, what do you mean exactly?"

Edward explained. "We look at what would have happened if Prince Charlie had stayed to fight another battle and if Flora Macdonald hadn't helped him escape. We could show how either of those things would have been a disaster."

"Yes!" Caitlin said. She put her hands on Edward's shoulders and shook him gently, before hugging him. "Oh, Ed, that *is* brilliant! We not only get the project done, but we get our proof put together for the Prince and Flora. I can't wait to get started!" She released a bewildered-looking Edward, and clasped her hands together and bounced up and down on her chair.

"Okay," Lynette said, taking a piece of paper from the pocket of her jeans. "Let's look at the mind map Mr Carnie gave us and draw up a plan."

Over the next two weeks, the three of them read books from the school library, looked on the internet, and, of course, double checked the information they found there.

Caitlin told Bella about the project and how they hoped to use it. Bella had been impressed and thought it was a perfect idea. She reassured Caitlin that this would definitely be time well spent.

They also asked Mr Carnie for advice. He said they were right about Bonnie Prince Charlie being a hero to Scottish people, and he also said that most historians agreed that it was a good thing Charlie didn't stay and fight on. He said it was almost certain that had the Prince stayed and undertaken another battle, he would have been defeated and put to death and that he would have been remembered as a failure.

He gave them the titles of some books about Bonnie Prince Charlie. Caitlin made sure they borrowed these books from the school library so they could take them with them when they went to see the Prince. Mr Carnie also said that it was heroes like Bonnie Prince Charlie that kept Scottish people proud and kept them determined to get a parliament back in Scotland, something they'd achieved in 1997. He said that the Prince had had to use his head and his heart in making his decision to leave and that in the end he had to do what was best for Scotland. Their teacher had praised the three of them for the effort they were putting into their project. Caitlin wondered what he'd think if he knew *why* they were putting in so much effort.

As well as speaking to their teacher, Caitlin organised a consultation with Granny Skye. She'd had a long face-to-face-time—as her grandmother called it—phone conversation with Granny just before the end of the holidays. Bella had suggested it and had also spoken to Granny. With

Granny being a Seer, it meant Caitlin could talk freely about going back to 1746. It had been wonderful for Caitlin to tell Granny Skye all about it and to discuss with Granny what it all meant. It was also lovely for Caitlin to talk about her mother also being a Seer.

On the Saturday at the end of the third week of high school, Lynette and Edward joined Caitlin in her bedroom for another face-to-face-time call to Granny Skye.

Caitlin began by telling her granny all about the history project and about how they hoped to use it on their return mission to 1746.

Caitlin's granny was able to tell them all about Flora Macdonald. She said she would take Caitlin to see Flora's cottage on Skye on the next occasion Caitlin was there. She was surprised that Caitlin didn't remember being taken there before, but when they worked out that Caitlin would only have been about six at the time, Granny said that explained it. She told them how brave Flora had been, how she hid the Prince in her house on the island of Uist and then disguised him as her maid-servant and accompanied him on the escape by boat to Skye where a ship to France and freedom awaited him.

She also reminded them about the Skye Boat Song and that they should sing it to the Prince if they got the chance. Caitlin had known the Skye Boat Song since she was tiny. Her mother used to sing it to her as a lullaby. But it was only now that the words made any real sense. Lynette and Edward also knew the song because Miss Stewart had taught it to the class for them to sing at the leavers' concert, but even then they hadn't paid that much attention to what they were actually singing about. It had just been some old, traditional song.

Granny Skye also told them that Flora was captured by the Redcoats for what she did and that she was sent to prison in London. However, she was later freed and settled back on Skye where she married and had children. She said that Flora should be very proud of her bravery, and that the children should be sure to tell her how people still admired her two hundred and sixty years later.

"I knew I'd picked the right time to give you the locket," Granny said to Caitlin. "Be sure and take it with you and give it to the Prince when you meet him. Tell him how you got it and that he's to give it to Flora as a token of his gratitude. That way if you find the locket safe and sound in your bedroom when you get back you'll know everything played out as it should."

"Oh yes," Caitlin said. "The locket will act as a sort of proof. Proof for the Prince, and then proof for us when we get back."

"Exactly," Granny said.

Before they said goodbye, Granny told Caitlin how proud she was of her and how proud Caitlin's mother would have been. This gave Caitlin a bit of a lump in her throat and tummy. Granny also said that Caitlin and her friends should be very proud of themselves for what they'd done and were about to do. Granny finished up by wishing them all good luck and said she'd keep in touch with Bella once their return mission to 1746 was underway.

As well as all their other preparations, the children also spent a Saturday morning at the museum where they bought a brochure and some postcards. The brochure told the story of Bonnie Prince Charlie and the postcards showed paintings of Flora and of the Prince.

On the afternoon of the Friday before the Monday deadline set by their teacher, they were finished. The project was complete and Caitlin, Lynette and Edward sat round the kitchen table at Caitlin's house, checking the book over.

"We've done a lot," Edward said, as he flicked through it.

"My mum's amazed how hard I've worked on this," Lynette

said. "She said she'd never seen me so keen on homework."

"You didn't say anything, did you, about why you were so keen?" Caitlin asked.

"Of course not," Lynette said. "She wouldn't have believed me even if I had."

Bella joined them in the kitchen. Since school had gone back, she no longer had to be at Caitlin's during the school day, but she was always at the house by four o'clock waiting for Caitlin to get back. When Caitlin told her their project was complete, Bella congratulated her and asked if she could see it.

"That's it," Bella said when she'd finished looking at what they'd written and at the history books and postcards and brochures they'd gathered. "With all this and the locket, you're bound to convince the Prince and Flora Macdonald."

"I hope so," Caitlin said. "When should we go?"

"I'll check it out," Bella said, "but I think tomorrow would be a good time."

Chapter Twenty One

Next morning, when Caitlin met her friends at the Hermitage, they looked a bit different to normal. Lynette had swapped her usual weekend jeans or leggings for plain black school trousers and instead of one of her pretty tops she had on a plain dark blue sweater. Her hair hadn't been straightened and it actually looked quite nice with its natural waves and curls. On her feet Lynette wore walking boots. Caitlin didn't even know she owned walking boots.

Lynette noticed Caitlin staring. "I thought I better blend in more," she said. "I borrowed the boots from Mum. I take the same size as her now. And this is the awful jumper my gran knitted for me. Mum thought I must be ill, insisted on taking my temperature before I left. I told her we were planning a long walk. That made her even more suspicious. But she seemed to think if you and Edward were going it would be okay."

Edward was dressed in his usual unremarkable jeans and sweatshirt but he'd added a tartan scarf, a Royal Stuart tartan scarf and he clutched the project book under his arm.

Caitlin had the library books and the brochures and postcards in her backpack. She too wore black jeans and black boots. She was also wearing the beret-type hat that Granny had sent to her. It was made of Cameron tartan and granny said the hat's proper name was its Scottish one. It was a Tam O' Shanter, or tammy for short. And Caitlin remembered that Ewen wore one.

"Good," Edward said looking at the girls. "Hopefully we'll not look quite so out of place this time."

Bella had also approved of how Caitlin looked when they'd said their goodbyes earlier. "You'll do," she'd said smiling at Caitlin. Then she'd hugged her. "Farewell, little Time Changer," she said. "Be brave and do what needs to be done."

"I will," Caitlin replied, and surprised herself and Bella by hugging Bella back very tightly. Bella stroked Caitlin's hair back from her face and looked into her eyes. She rubbed Caitlin's back with her free hand in a way that made Caitlin think of her mother. Caitlin felt like laughing and crying at the same time. She also felt all mixed up about going on this mission. Part of her was excited and keen to get started, and part of her just wanted to stay where she was and be cuddled by Bella.

Caitlin also said goodbye to Jack Russell. Bella had told Caitlin that it had been decided that Jack shouldn't accompany her this time. "My boss feels that there will be enough people in the know and looking after you to rule out the need for any long messages. The birds will be a safer means of communicating, and not having Jack with you means you'll have one less thing to think about."

"Who is your boss?" Caitlin asked. "You haven't told us anything about the Invigilator who's in charge of all this."

Bella smiled. "Not now," she said. "When you get back, I'll tell you all about the boss then." Bella gave her one last quick squeeze and stepped back. She cleared her throat and blinked hard a couple of times before saying, "Okay, you better be going."

By ten o'clock, Caitlin, Lynette and Edward were standing beside the ice house, with their backs to the big, old granny pine.

"If it's like last time we should sit close together and lean against the trunk of the tree," said Caitlin, checking her tammy was secure on her head.

The other two nodded.

"Let's do it!" Lynette said. They sat down at the base of the tree and then leaned back and pressed their palms against the trunk. For a moment nothing happened. Then the birds went quiet and they all felt themselves begin to tumble. Down and back they fell, like before, until, with a thud, they landed.

The three of them got quickly to their feet. They looked around. They were in wood, a familiar wood, below a familiar tree.

"We're in the right place," Lynette said. This is where Lucy brought us. Here's hoping we've arrived at the right time."

"Where do we go from here?" Lynette asked.

"To Achnaharrie?" Caitlin suggested, "like Locheil told us to."

"Yes, but how? Can you remember the way?" Lynette asked, looking around.

Edward reached into the pocket of his jeans and produced a piece of paper. "Memory map," he said.

Caitlin remembered how he'd been taking notes as Lucy had led them to the spot where they were now. She smiled as she realised what he'd been up to. "You used your notes to make a map," she said. "This memory map stuff, it really is like you told Craig and Corinna, it's your new grown-up version of the mapsticks."

"I suppose it is," Edward said.

"Let's see," Lynette said, looking over Edward's shoulder. Edward held out the map so Lynette and Caitlin could look at it.

It had lots on it. Edward had drawn all the trees, the rowan, birches and ash, that lined the track they were standing on, including the different colours and patterns of the bark of these trees. He said he'd put in the details about the bark because if they returned in a different season there may be no leaves to recognise the trees by. And he'd been right to do so. Judging by the amount of fallen leaves at their feet, it was no longer the spring of 1746.

He'd also drawn a squirrel much further along the track at the point where he'd seen one on their walk with Lucy and Ewen. He said that was because he would look for signs of squirrel activity at that point on their way back, as a check that they were on the right path. For similar reasons he'd also drawn the site of a large rookery that they'd passed.

"Here's where we turn off the track onto the gravel road that leads to Achnaharrie," Edward said pointing. "There's a big sandstone rock at the road end. Remember, where we rested?"

The girls nodded.

"And there it is on my map," Edward said, indicating his drawing of the rock.

There were lots more similar details on Edward's map, including arrows to show the way and whether it was going up or downhill, and the distances were recorded as the number of Edward-length paces.

"I don't think we'll get lost using this," Caitlin said. "It's excellent, Ed."

"So, let's go," Lynette said, beginning to walk in the direction shown on the map.

"Yep," Edward said , as he and Caitlin followed.

With such an accurate map to guide them, it didn't take long to reach the gates of Achnaharrie. But even before they got there, Caitlin sensed there was something very wrong. And the closer they got the more certain she became. It was eerily quiet, and there was that smell, that unmistakable smell of burning.

Caitlin and the others would never forget what they saw that day as they stood at Achnaharrie's wide open gates. All that remained of the house was rubble. Smoke still rose from the smouldering remains of the building. Caitlin, Edward and Lynette gasped and looked at each other.

"What do you think happened?" Caitlin asked. "I mean, I can see it's burned down but how, why?"

"Redcoats," Edward said. "Redcoats, looking for Locheil and the family. They either burnt them out, or did this as a punishment, or maybe a warning. It's all gone. The house, the stables, everything."

Caitlin shivered. "Perhaps we should go and take a look round?"

"Yes," Lynette said. "But we'd better keep out of sight. Whoever did this could still be nearby."

Edward removed his tartan scarf and put it in his duffle bag. "You should hide that too," he said pointing at Caitlin's tammy. She quickly stuffed it into her backpack.

"Right," Lynette said, and she beckoned to the other two to follow her. They made for the trees at the side of the driveway.

The three of them then walked towards the remains of the house. At the top of the driveway, Lynette looked out from behind the last tree. She nodded to the others and put her finger to her lips. They walked towards what was left of the house, right up to where the front door had once been. There was no sign of life as they walked around the ruins. Here and there part of a wall remained, jutting upwards, but mostly it was just rubble. None of them spoke until they'd gone all the way round.

They stood in shock for a moment then Lynette said, "Do you think the family got away?"

"And what's it to you if they did or they didn't?" said a voice behind them.

All three of them jumped and spun round.

Two men in white breeches and red jackets stood looking at them. They carried rifles with bayonets attached. Rifles that were now pointed at Caitlin, Lynette and Edward.

Chapter Twenty Two

Caitlin's heart beat very fast and very hard. She trembled with fear. Redcoats! She glanced at Lynette and Edward. Lynette had gone pale and she reached for Caitlin's hand. Edward stood straight and appeared calm.

The soldier who'd spoken circled the little group, looking them up and down. He was small and thin with a pointed face and he reminded Caitlin of a weasel. The other soldier moved forward and pushed the point of his bayonet towards Caitlin. "My comrade asked you a question, boy," he said. He smiled a horrible smile. Caitlin noticed he had very bad teeth and very bad breath.

Edward stepped forward and, as he did so, he pushed Caitlin and Lynette behind him. "It's nothing to us. We were just curious, that's all."

"Uh huh," said the soldier with the bad teeth, glancing at his companion who was now standing beside him. "Names," he said.

"Names? Oh you mean our names—what are our names?" Edward said.

"Yes, what group of Highland scum do you belong to?" Bad Teeth said. Caitlin was shocked to hear his Scottish accent, an Edinburgh accent. So it was true. Not all the Redcoats were English. Bad teeth spoke again, "Not Camerons, I hope." He poked Edward on the arm with the bayonet. His comrade laughed.

"What us?" Edward said. "Camerons? No, no we're—

we're Farquharsons—me and my—my brothers. I'm Edward and they are C-Colin and L-Liam."

"So, Edward and C-Colin and L-Liam what brings you here?" Bad Teeth poked Edward again, this time in the stomach. Edward moved back. The weasely one laughed.

"We—we're from the village. We were looking for food. Our supplies are running low," Edward said.

"Uh huh," Bad Teeth said. "From the village? Is that right? So, how come you didn't know the house was burned down and there'd be no food here?"

"I—we—I—"

Weasel was running out of patience. "Ach," he said. "We should just kill them and get on our way." He put the tip of his bayonet at Edward's throat.

"Please, don't kill us," Edward said, raising his hands and backing off still further. He pushed his back against Caitlin and Lynette and they scuttled behind a bush, where they cowered, clinging to one another. Weasel laughed, watching them.

"Please, we didn't know," Edward went on. "We were so scared. We've been hiding for ages. We didn't know about the house. We're just looking for food."

"You don't sound as if you're from round here," Bad Teeth said. "I'd say you have an Edinburgh way of speaking."

"Come up to fight for the Prince, did you, for the lost cause?" Weasel said.

"No, no, we didn't come to fight. And you're right we *are* from Edinburgh. We were visiting our uncle in the village, and then the battle happened and we couldn't get home."

"Enough!" Bad Teeth shouted. "Let's just kill them and get back to camp." He grabbed hold of Caitlin and Lynette and dragged them out from behind the bush. He raised his bayonet and pointed it at Lynette's chest.

Caitlin screamed as Edward stepped in front of Lynette. Bad Teeth snarled and pushed Edward to the ground.

"Run!" Edward shouted, but Lynette was frozen with fear. Weasel grabbed her, bayonet raised. Caitlin wanted to run but couldn't bring herself to leave Lynette and Edward.

And then, as Edward rolled over on the ground to avoid Bad Teeth's boot, a loud siren-like noise sounded. Several, urgent, short, trumpet-like notes travelled on the air. They came from somewhere behind where the house had once stood.

Weasel lowered his bayonet, and Bad Teeth's boot stopped in midair. The two Redcoats looked at each other. "Bugle call," Weasel said. "Company's striking camp."

"Come on," Bad Teeth said. "We don't want to be last. We'll end up on foot and carrying all the kit."

"What about these?" Weasel said, nodding at Caitlin and the others.

The trumpet sound came again.

"Leave them," Bad Teeth replied. "They're just stupid children. Not worth being late for." And with that, the two Redcoats scuttled off down the drive.

Edward, Caitlin and Lynette stood watching them. For a few moments nobody spoke. Then Caitlin ran at Edward and flung her arms around him. He hugged her back. "Oh, Edward," Caitlin said. " You were so brave. Are you okay?"

"Yes, yes," he said. "I'm fine." He stretched out an arm towards Lynette who looked dazed. "Lynette?" he said.

Caitlin also turned to her friend. "Lynette," she said softly. "Come here." She too stretched out an arm towards her.

Lynette looked at them both for a moment and then stumbled into their arms. The three of them clung together.

There was the sound of a throat being cleared and then an unmistakable snort and whinny. The three of them turned from their embrace. There beside them were Angus and Hero. Angus grinned at them and waved the brass instrument that he was wearing on a cord round his neck. He seemed to be fully recovered from his wounds.

Caitlin gasped and said, "What? How? The trumpet noise, was that you?"

"It's a bugle," Angus said. "And, yes, it was me."

"But how? Where did you and Hero come from?" Caitlin said.

"I was here, hiding," Angus said. "I was waiting for you. Locheil got word to me at Kincraig when he realised he and his family would have to make a run for it. He asked me to come and wait for you. He was sure it wouldn't be long before you arrived. I found Hero in the woods and we hid up the hill at the back to watch out for you arriving. I found the bugle in the rubble. It must have been dropped by the raiding party that set fire to this place. And I had the idea of using it to lure that pair of thugs away."

"Brilliant!" Lynette said.

Caitlin felt light-headed with relief. "Well, it certainly worked. The Redcoats seemed to think they were being summoned back to camp."

"It won't be long before they work out it was a trick," Edward said. "I think we better get moving."

"Yes, you're right," Angus said. "They're camped close by, about twenty of them. They've been rounding up anyone they think fought against them and burning homes and crops. And of course they're looking for the Prince." Angus turned to Caitlin. "Locheil's in hiding and Ewen and Lucy are with him. It's his intention to meet up with Prince Charlie. He sent me with two horses and I've to take you to him."

"Will it be safe?" Caitlin asked. She stroked Hero's head and neck as she spoke and the horse nuzzled her. "And do you know where we're to go?"

"We'll have to be careful of course," Angus said. "But we should be safe and we won't get lost."

"How can you be so sure?" Lynette asked.

"Because Murdo's on his way to join us," Angus said, smiling. "He'll be leading us to Rannoch Moor to Locheil and the Prince."

"Excellent!" Caitlin said.

"Brilliant!" Lynette said.

"That's good," Edward said.

Angus took them back into the woods where they'd arrived earlier. Edward led Hero. They went much further in than the site of the granny pine to a place where the trees were so close together that very little light got through. Then, just as their eyes were adjusting to the semi-darkness, they emerged into a small clearing.

Two horses were tethered to a tree and Angus took Hero over to join them. Then he lifted the low branches of a willow and beckoned to the others. They all ducked under the branches and found themselves beside a makeshift shelter. It consisted of sheepskins and other animal hides roughly sewn together and these were draped across the gap between two tall trees. The skins provided a roof and three sides. The ground underneath was also covered in sheepskins.

"Welcome to my home," Angus said, smiling. "I've been hiding out here for a couple of days, awaiting your arrival."

"Will we be setting off right away?" Lynette asked. "What time is it anyway? My stomach says it's nearly lunchtime, but that's on the twenty-first century clock."

"And what's the date?" Edward asked. "How long have we been away from 1746?"

"It's September," said a man's voice. "You've been gone five months, and it's lunchtime here too."

"Murdo!" said Caitlin, Lynette and Edward together.

Murdo grinned and gave a little bow. "Hello, young friends. It's good to see you again."

Two more men appeared behind Murdo as he spoke. They led three more horses. The animals were laden with supplies.

"Yes!" Lynette said. "It's Hector and Norman."

The two men smiled and waved and made their way over to join the rest of them.

Murdo pointed at them as they approached. "Locheil said I was to bring my two best men for this journey, but they weren't available, so I brought these two clowns instead." He laughed as he dodged punches from Hector and Norman. The children laughed too.

It was Caitlin who got them back to more serious matters. "Is it far to Rannoch Moor?" she said. "To where Locheil is?"

"Aye, it's a day's ride," Murdo replied. "So I reckon we should have something to eat now and then get on our way. We'll camp out tonight and finish our journey tomorrow."

Murdo and the men unpacked some chicken and bread, and some flasks of water. As they did so, a thought struck Caitlin. She looked in her backpack. Yes! Bella had done it again. Three foil packages were nestled at the bottom of the bag, along with three cartons of apple juice and a packet of milk chocolate digestives. The packages were labeled with the children's names.

"I thought my bag was a bit heavy," Caitlin said, as she handed out the food to her friends.

"Yes!" Lynette said, when she unwrapped her sandwiches. "Cheese and pickle is my absolute favourite."

"I've got my favourite too," Caitlin said. "Yummy tuna mayo. What have you got Ed?"

"Cheddar cheese with strawberry jam," Edward said.

"What?" Lynette gasped. "Cheese and jam. How weird is that?"

"It's not weird. I like it," Edward said. "It's no weirder than cheese and tomato. After all tomato is a fruit too. It's a nutritious and tasty combination and the jam brings out the full flavour of the cheese."

"Whatever," Lynette said, rolling her eyes.

Caitlin laughed. Even in this very strange situation, Edward and Lynette were behaving exactly as they would at any other time. She silently thanked Bella, not just for the food, but for helping to keep things sort of normal.

A short time later, their hunger and thirst satisfied, the party were on their way. Caitlin rode on Hero with Lynette while Edward shared a horse with Angus.

As on their previous journey with Murdo, they kept under cover as much as possible. And in spite of the possible danger, Caitlin was pleased to be riding Hero again.

It also felt good to be with Murdo again. She wondered how much he knew of their mission, if he knew about the existence of Time Keepers, Seers and Time Changers. Was he simply a loyal servant who did as his clan leader told him without question? Or had he, like Angus and Ewen, been granted Need-to-Know status?

Caitlin's head was so full of thoughts that their time on the road seemed to pass very quickly. Before she knew it, they were dismounting at the edge of some moorland in the shelter of a few pine trees and gorse bushes.

Hector and Norman fed and watered the horses while Murdo made a fire with fallen tree branches, and Angus set out his animal skins for the party to sleep on. Dinner was potatoes and some very salty meat, washed down with strong tea served in tin mugs. As they all had a second mugful of tea, Caitlin passed round the remaining chocolate digestives. Hector was most impressed by the biscuits and asked Caitlin how to make them, so he could tell his Morag. Edward saved Caitlin from having to explain by saying it was a secret family recipe.

After the meal, Lynette and Edward sat with Hector and Norman and listened to more tall tales of the men's many adventures.

Caitlin found herself at the opposite side of the fire, sitting in between Murdo and Angus. The three of them sat on a tartan blanket which Murdo had spread on the ground. As usual they talked in a mix of Gaelic and English, Gaelic to each other and English to Caitlin. Caitlin liked the sound of the Gaelic, especially as it reminded her of her grandparents and of Skye. She was glad that it hadn't died out completely after Culloden. She also thought how brave the people had been who'd kept the language alive and who'd continued to wear tartan, even after both were outlawed.

"Isn't it dangerous to be seen with tartan?" she asked. "You're both still wearing it and this plaid we're sitting on, haven't the Hanoverians outlawed it, those two Redcoats that caught us at Achnaharrie—?"

"Were traitors," Murdo said. "Two Scotsmen, turncoat traitors both. We'll never give up the tartan or our language. They can make as many laws as they like." Murdo jumped to his feet and kicked the trunk of the nearest tree, a deep frown on his face. He strode away from the fire. He looked so angry that Caitlin cowered slightly.

Angus put his hand on her arm. "Don't worry," he said. "Murdo barks loud but he doesn't bite. It's these new laws. They make him wild. And as for Scots who fight in Cumberland's army, that really chokes him."

Caitlin tried to smile. "It's strange that Scottish people would fight for the Hanoverians. I was surprised when I found that out."

Angus shook his head. "Yes, I know. It's confusing. And there are plenty Englishmen and French who fight on Prince Charlie's side."

"It all seems very complicated," Caitlin said. "I wonder why everyone can't just get along."

"So, in the twenty-first century, are things simpler? Do people get along? Have the Scots and the English, and all the other countries in the world sorted out their differences?"

"Not exactly," Caitlin said. "There's still fighting and wars I'm afraid. Although Scotland doesn't fight with England, and Scotland does have its own parliament again. That's something, I suppose."

"Really!" Angus said.

"Yes," Caitlin said, "but the world's still far from perfect."

Just then Murdo came back. "We should all get some rest," he said "Sorry," he said to Caitlin. "Sorry for getting angry. It's just things are so—so—"

"Complicated? Infuriating? Unjust?" Caitlin suggested.

"Yes, all of those," Murdo said. He smiled at her. "You're very wise, for one so young."

Caitlin smiled back. She felt proud to have Murdo's admiration. It was like when her father told her he was proud of her.

"Right give me a hand here," Murdo said. And together they began to tidy up. She helped Murdo to pick up the plates and mugs and they gave them to Angus who rinsed them in the burn. Murdo then kicked dirt onto the fire to put it out.

Hector and Norman checked on the horses, and Caitlin and Lynette went off to the edge of their camping spot to find a suitably private spot for their toilet needs. Caitlin smiled at Lynette's renewed protests at the lack of modern plumbing. They washed their hands and faces in the icy burn and this drew more grumbling from Lynette.

When they rejoined the others, everyone except Murdo was already lying down wrapped in their plaids and sheepskins.

"The men have left you both the spot at the back, under the big tree," Murdo said. "Go and get settled for the night."

"What about you?" Lynette asked.

"I'm on first watch," Murdo said. "Hector and Norman will take their turns later."

"Right," Lynette said turning to go. "Good night, then."

"Good night," Murdo said. "You should go too, miss," he said to Caitlin. "You have an important day tomorrow. Things will always be complicated, unjust and infuriating, but at least people like you ensure they turn out as they're meant to, and, it is to be hoped, for the best."

Caitlin looked at Murdo. He knew. She looked into his

eyes and she knew that he knew. He looked back at her and gave the slightest of nods.

As Caitlin fell asleep that night, Murdo's words came back to her and she hoped she'd be able to live up to his faith in her. Could she really influence events and keep history on track?

Chapter Twenty Three

It was just after noon when the group arrived at the edge of Rannoch Moor. The moor was vast and rose to a plateau at its centre. It would be easy for enemy troops to set up a lookout and spot any travellers on the boggy expanse.

They stopped to eat, but Murdo was uneasy about them being so exposed so they were soon on their way again.

Murdo rode at the head of the group. Hector and Norman brought up the rear. The ground was heather-covered peat bog and the going was slow.

As they rode along, Caitlin looked at the high mountain which dominated the moor's north-western corner.

Murdo pointed at the mountain. "The Buchaille Etive Mhor," Murdo said, over his shoulder. "That's where Locheil is hiding out, in the shelter of the Buchaille."

They followed the course of the River Etive, passing several small lochans along the way. It was about another hour before they came into the shadow of the pyramid-shaped mountain, and, as they got close to its base, they could just make out a small stone building squatting there. It seemed to be made out of the same grey stone as the mountain itself and was therefore well camouflaged until you got very near.

Murdo led them round to the back of the shelter and they all dismounted. A burn flowed down from the mountain and along behind the building. The far side of the burn was forest, Caledonian pine forest, according to Edward.

Several horses were tethered to a couple of rough posts

and a wooden cart stood propped against the back wall of the hut. Hector and Norman took the group's horses to the burn. The animals drank while the men prepared their feed. Meanwhile the others made their way to the front of the building and Murdo tapped out a rhythmic knock on the door.

A voice from inside called out in Gaelic. Murdo replied, also in Gaelic.

The door opened a crack and then was flung wide. Ewen stood there smiling. "Come in, friends. Come in!" he said.

They all crowded into the little building. The only light inside filtered in through a small slit in the back wall. There seemed to be just the one room, furnished only with some wooden chairs, a table and a rough bench. Through the gloom, as her eyes adjusted to the low light, Caitlin could make out a figure on a chair in the corner and there also appeared to be someone standing alongside.

Then someone spoke and moved out of the shadows and towards the group of new arrivals.

It was Lucy."You came back!" she said. She came straight to Caitlin and hugged her and then also embraced Lynette and even Edward, despite his squirming. She called over her shoulder, "Father, they came back, they came back!"

A deep laugh came from the seated figure in the corner. "I don't know why you're so surprised at their return. It was you who told me that they were on their way. Come here everyone. Let me see you all."

At this point, Murdo excused himself to go and check that Hector and Norman had got the horses secured and to unload the bags and supplies they'd brought with them. Ewen and Lucy went with him.

Lynette, Edward, Caitlin, and Angus went over to Locheil.

"It is good to see you all again," Locheil said. "Well done, Angus. Did your meeting with these fine young people go well?"

Angus and Edward exchanged glances.

"There was a slight hitch, sir," Angus said.

"But it was soon sorted out," Edward said.

"How are your wounds?" Caitlin asked.

"Much better," Locheil said. "I can walk, as long as I use this." He pointed to the wooden stick that lay against his chair.

"And your house," Caitlin said. "I'm so sorry that it got burnt down."

Locheil looked sad and shook his head. "Yes, it was a terrible thing to happen. And I'm sorry it meant that we couldn't be there to meet you when you came back."

"Oh, that's all right," Caitlin said. "Angus and Murdo and the men looked after us."

Locheil nodded. "So, tell me, did you get what is needed?"

"Yes, I think so," Caitlin said. "We have a—a document that we've put together. It has all sorts of proof, and we have books and pictures, and even a song about the Prince."

There was movement from the opposite corner of the room and a tall man emerged from the darkness.

"A song? A song about me?" The man looked at Caitlin. He spoke with a strange accent. Caitlin thought he sounded French. She also thought he was very handsome. She couldn't help staring. She looked him up and down. His blonde hair was drawn back in a ponytail and he wore a tartan jacket and white breeches and stockings. On his feet he had silver-buckled black shoes. And she knew who he was immediately.

Bonnie Prince Charlie certainly lived up to his name.

"He's gorgeous!" Lynette whispered in Caitlin's ear.

Locheil struggled to his feet and shuffled forward to stand at the Prince's side. "Your Highness," he said. "This is Miss Caitlin Cameron. The young lady I told you about."

"Indeed!" said the Prince. "Mademoiselle," he said, inclining his head slightly towards Caitlin.

Caitlin gave a little curtsey and looked at the floor. She didn't know what was more embarrassing, meeting a Prince, and such a famous one at that, or the fact that she'd been mentioned to him.

Locheil continued, "And this is Miss Lynette Maclean and Mr Edward Farquharson."

Lynette giggled and also gave a curtsey. Edward bowed his head.

"Miss Cameron," said the Prince, "I understand from Locheil that you and your companions come from the future. I must say if it was anyone other than my good friend, telling me this fantastic story, I wouldn't believe them. I also understand that you come with advice, urgent advice, and that I need to listen to it."

Caitlin's mouth went dry. She put her hand on the strap of her rucksack, thinking of its important contents. This was all way too weird. She glanced round. Lynette had a soppy grin on her face. Edward's head was still bowed. Even Angus seemed overawed.

It was Locheil who broke the silence. "Perhaps if we all sit down, then Caitlin can tell you her story?"

"Of course," the Prince said.

Soon the group were settled at the far end of the room. Locheil sat in his chair and the Prince perched on a stool, leaning forward, his elbows on his knees, and his chin resting on his hands, as he prepared to listen. Caitlin and her friends made themselves as comfortable as they could on the floor, sitting on the blanket rolls that Murdo had brought in.

And, as Murdo and the men came and went, and Lucy and Ewen prepared a meal for them all, Caitlin began her mission to convince Bonnie Prince Charlie what he must do.

But the group inside the hut hardly noticed what the others were up to as Caitlin, helped by her friends, told how the Jacobite story played out down the years. Caitlin showed the Prince the history books, brochures and pictures they'd brought with them as well as, of course, the project book they'd made.

Prince Charlie listened intently. He scrutinised the books, read the project notes, studied the photos of the portraits of him in the brochures and on the postcards.

Before Caitlin could mention the escape plan, Lucy came to say that dinner was ready.

The Prince nodded at Lucy and then turned back to Caitlin. "You've given me much to think about," he said. "Let us eat and I will consider all that you have shared with me."

Lucy helped her father to his feet. "Murdo lit a fire outside for us to cook on. It's at the back. He says it won't be seen and that we'll be more comfortable outdoors while we eat.

Soon everyone had found a spot to sit and eat their hearty platefuls of stew. The moon rose in the dusky sky and the evening air was cool and fresh. The fire crackled, a curlew called, and all around them the birch, alder and Scots pine trees creaked and whispered.

The Prince and Locheil sat to one side on the seats that had been carried outside for them. Murdo and the men sat on their unrolled plaids at the far end of the enclosed area. And the six young people sat in a group near the corner of the hut, some perched on small rocks others sitting on their blankets or jackets.

"What do you think Prince Charlie will do?" Lynette asked.

The boys scarcely looked up, more interested in eating their meal than in speculating about what would happen next.

"He'll do what's right," Lucy said. "I'm sure of it. How could he not after what you three just told him?"

Caitlin hoped Lucy was right. She felt such a responsibility. If she hadn't managed to convince the Prince to flee to France, then history would change and Scotland could face a very different future. And she'd have failed as a Time Changer. She laid down her plate, no longer hungry.

Lynette squeezed her arm. "Don't worry," she said. "You did just fine."

"Can I have that?" Ewen asked, reaching to pick up Caitlin's plate.

"Ewen!" Lucy gasped. "Where are your manners? Of course you can't!" She turned to Caitlin. "Sorry about him. Don't pay any heed."

"What?" Ewen said. "If Caitlin doesn't want it, why can't I have it?"

Lucy frowned. "Because it's not appropriate, not seemly. Can't you see that Caitlin's worried? Have you no sensitivity?"

Ewen looked baffled. Angus shook his head and grinned at him.

"Tut, tut," Angus said to him. "Have you no finer feelings, laddie?"

"I don't see a problem," Edward said. "If the food's just going to be binned, why can't he have it?"

Caitlin started to laugh. They all looked at her. "Have it," she said pushing her plate towards Ewen, who scooped it up and immediately began eating.

"What are you laughing at?" Edward asked.

"Oh, I don't know," Caitlin said. "It's just the way we all are." She swept her arm round the group. You wouldn't think we're normally separated by more than two hundred and fifty years. We could all be in the canteen at school."

It was while Caitlin, Edward, and Lynette were in the middle of debating whether they should explain school and canteen to the other three that they were interrupted by Murdo.

He spoke to Caitlin. "The Prince would like to hear the song you spoke of," he said.

"Oh, right," Caitlin said.

Edward jumped up. "I'll go and get the words," he said.

By the time he came back everyone had gathered around the fire, some sitting, some standing.

As she prepared to sing with her two friends, Caitlin felt her mum was very close.

"After three," Lynette said. "One, two, three."

The three of them began to sing. *'Speed bonny boat, like a bird on the wing, onward the sailors cry. Carry the lad that's born to be king, over the sea to Skye...'*

The Prince, again, appeared to listen closely as the song's words described the battle at Culloden, the Prince's daring escape across the sea, and the promise that Charlie would come again.

When the song was finished, Edward handed Prince Charlie the sheet music and the words. The Prince took a few moments to read the song's words, its chorus and verses.

"Again!" he said. "Sing it again!"

So Caitlin and her friends sang it again, and this time some of the men began to hum along.

When it ended for a second time, the Prince had tears in his eyes, as did Locheil.

"Of course," said Caitlin. "The words aren't quite true because as we've shown you, you

aren't meant to get the chance to *actually* come again. But in a way it *is* true because as far as

Scottish history is concerned you've never really left, never been forgotten. People have

come back to the memory of you again and again."

"Excuse me," the Prince said. "I must think." He walked away from them and went

indoors.

The group began to drift away from the campfire. Hector and Norman went to check on the horses. Ewen and Lucy gathered up plates and spoons and took them to the burn to wash them. Murdo and Angus doused the fire and then, with daggers drawn, went to check that nobody lurked in the nearby bushes, or behind the various large, granite boulders scattered about. Only Caitlin and her two friends remained sitting by the embers, along with Locheil.

"So," Locheil said. "What's the plan, if the Prince agrees?"

"He must escape to France," Caitlin said. "The history books say that if he had stayed to fight on, he'd have been defeated. The Jacobites were scattered and too many had died for there to be any chance of success. His escape meant it wasn't a complete defeat. He remained a hero to the Scots right up until our time."

Locheil nodded. "And how will he get to France?"

"There's a boat waiting for him. It's tied up at the island of Benbecula off the west coast. Things won't go smoothly but he will eventually get safely away with the help of a woman named Flora Macdonald, first to Uist and then to Skye, and from there to France."

"And how does the Prince get on in France?" asked Locheil.

"I—well—I don't—I can't—"

"Stop interrogating the girl, Locheil." The Prince had returned. "I'm sure she's not supposed to reveal more than is absolutely necessary in order to keep history on track. Am I right, Miss Cameron?"

"Yes, Your Highness, you're right," Caitlin said.

"No man should know his entire fate. But I know what I must do next. I've thought about all that you've said, Miss Cameron, and about how my going means that all hope will not be lost. I can see I was foolish to think I could fight on, for the moment, at least. So, how do I get to Uist?"

"Murdo and the men will escort you to the coast," Caitlin said. "There you will meet a Captain O'Neill who'll see you safely to the island. But, because there'll be lots of Redcoats in residence, you'll need to make your way from there to the Isle of Skye with the help of the woman Flora Macdonald.

She and the captain will ensure you get to your ship for France."

The Prince nodded. He looked very serious for a moment. Then he smiled. He stepped forward and hugged first Caitlin, and then Lynette and Edward. All three children were too stunned to speak.

Prince Charlie stepped back and looked at them. "What brave young souls, to travel so far to bring me this wise advice. It has been an honour to meet you, young Time Changer, you and your companions. Thank you." He bowed low before them.

It was Edward who recovered first. "It was an honour for us, Your Highness, to meet you and to try to help. But it was Caitlin who did the most. Lynette and me, we just sort of kept her company."

"Everyone needs true and loyal friends beside them, Master Farquharson. It is certainly true for me and I'm sure it is so for Miss Cameron."

Caitlin nodded at the Prince and at Edward.

"Oh," Caitlin said, reaching into the pocket of her trousers. "I almost forgot." She brought out the box containing the silver locket. She opened the box and held it out to the Prince. He listened as Caitlin explained its significance.

"So I should tell this Flora Macdonald all that you have told me, about her historic heroism and bravery in order to convince her to help me, and I should give her this necklace as a thank you from me to her," the Prince said.

"Yes, exactly," Caitlin said.

"I will leave in the morning," the Prince said. "But now let's go indoors. Locheil has told me we're to have a ceilidh."

And Locheil was true to his word. Once everyone was back inside the hut he told Murdo to play. Caitlin and her friends were amazed when Murdo produced a fiddle and began to play. He played reels and jigs and everyone clapped and stamped their feet. Lynette performed a few Highland dances and then Locheil and Prince Charlie watched as the rest of them danced Strip the Willow and the Eightsome Reel. The ceilidh ended with Lynette, Edward and Caitlin singing, 'Hey Johnnie Cope'. It was another traditional song that Miss Stewart had taught them, and another song whose words had again meant little when they first learned them. It commemorated the Prince's victory over the Hanoverian army at the battle of Prestonpans just the year before in 1745. It taunted the Hanoverian army's commander, Sir John Cope, and it brought a loud round of applause from the men, as well as a few tears to their eyes.

As Caitlin drifted off to sleep that night, curled up in her blue blanket on the hut floor, she thought this had been the most amazing night of her life.

Chapter Twenty Four

Next morning everyone woke early. But it was Murdo who was up first and had porridge made for everyone, by the time they were dressed.

He was keen for his group to be on their way, and as soon as they'd had breakfast, Hector and Norman loaded up the horses. Angus and Ewen also prepared for their journey. They would be going with Locheil and Lucy to a safe house in Inverness. Lucy busied herself getting her father and herself ready to leave.

Caitlin, Lynette and Edward packed up their project book, along with the library books and other stuff that they'd brought, apart from of course the silver locket, and then they went outside while everyone else made their preparations. Caitlin wanted to say goodbye to Hero. Prince Charlie would be riding him to the coast.

She approached the horse who was already saddled up and bearing several bags. He was tied loosely to a small rowan tree. He whinnied softly as she came near. He nuzzled her hand and she stroked his neck. "Goodbye," she whispered. "Thanks for everything. Carry the lad that's born to be king..." She wondered if she'd ever see Hero again and she wiped at a tear with the back of her hand. The horse whinnied once more.

Edward appeared at her side. "Hero says you've not to worry. Everything's going to be fine."

Caitlin looked from her friend to the horse, and she

found she believed Edward, believed that he knew what Hero was saying, and believed the words to be true. She gave Hero another pat. "Goodbye, my friend," she said.

Edward put his arm around her shoulders and the two of them stood for a moment looking into Hero's soft brown eyes.

Then Lynette came skipping up to them. "So, how do we get back?" she said.

Before Caitlin or Edward could answer her, Lucy called to them. "The Prince is ready to leave. He wants to say goodbye."

The three of them went back inside. Locheil was already saying his goodbyes to the Prince. Hector and Norman had gone to bring the horses round to the front.

"My young friends," the Prince said, turning to greet the children. "I'm leaving now and wanted to thank you again and to bid you adieu." He shook hands with all three of them.

"Good luck," Lynette said.

"All the best," Edward said.

"Be safe," Caitlin said.

And with a last nod at Locheil, the Prince turned to leave.

The others all followed him outside. He looked really handsome sitting on Hero's back. Hector and Norman were already mounted as well, one on each side of the Prince.

Murdo was holding his horse's reins. "Goodbye young Lowlanders," he said, smiling at the three friends.

Caitlin went up to him and hugged him. He looked surprised, but he hugged her back. "Thanks, Murdo," she said. "Thanks for everything."

Murdo smiled. "No, it is I who should be thanking you," he said. "You've made sure His Highness does the right thing." He swung up onto his horse. "I wish you Godspeed and a safe journey home."

And with that the Prince's party moved off. The others watched until they were out of sight.

"What now?" Lynette asked, as they turned to go indoors

once more. "How do we get home this time?"

"Don't worry about that," Ewen said. "My sister has it all worked out."

Lucy helped her father settle back into his chair and then stood behind it.

"Come and sit with us," Locheil said.

Caitlin, Lynette and Edward made themselves as comfy as they could sitting crosslegged on the floor. Ewen and Angus leant on the window sill to the side of Locheil's seat.

"Soon my children and I will begin our journey to our new home," Locheil said. "Angus will come with us and remain with us until we're sure it's safe for him to return to Kincraig. But first, Lucy and the young men will escort you to your departure point so that you too may go home." He looked round at them all. "You've done an excellent and very brave thing. And you, young Caitlin, you are a credit to all Time Changers, past, present and future."

"Thank you," Caitlin said. "I hoped I would be."

"You have saved Scotland's pride and the honour of the Jacobites. If the Prince had stayed to fight, all would have been lost. Instead the Jacobites can continue to offer resistance to King George but with no more bloodshed, for now, at least. And the Prince won't now be remembered as the person who brought an end to the Highland way of life, but as someone who gave hope. Well done, all of you."

"So, when do we go?" Edward asked.

"Now," Lucy said. "We must go now. We'll escort you to a nearby stand of ancient pines. One of them is your portal and it will open at noon."

After a final goodbye to Locheil, Caitlin and her companions set off east across the moor. Lucy led the way unerringly, even though she'd never been there before. It took about half an hour to get to a small ridge and, as they crested it, the party could see a little group of trees below.

"Looks like that's the place," Edward said.

Lucy, still striding ahead, called over her shoulder, "It is. That's the place."

Caitlin, Lynette and the lads had to stride out to keep up with Lucy on the descent.

Soon they entered the small copse of Scots pines. Birds chirped in their branches. In the centre stood one that was taller and thicker than the rest, the Granny.

Lucy went up to it and ran her hands over the bark. The sun was almost directly overhead. The birdsong stopped. "It's time," she said.

The young people embraced each other and said their farewells.

Caitlin squeezed Angus particularly tightly. "You take care," she said.

"Thank you so much, Caitlin. And thank you again for saving my life," he replied.

"Oh, you're very welcome," she replied, smiling. "When I saved you, I saved myself."

Angus looked at her, puzzled, as Lynette and Edward pushed her towards the tree. His quizzical expression was the last thing Caitlin saw as Lucy shouted, "Press hard!"

The next thing Caitlin knew she was falling, falling through time, back to the Hermitage in Edinburgh and back to the twenty-first century.

Chapter Twenty Five

As soon as they landed at the base of the pine tree, Edward checked his watch. "It's still Saturday, same day we went away, but it's now nearly lunchtime."

"And we certainly seem to be in the Hermitage," Lynette said as she looked back at the ice house and then down towards the Visitor Centre.

"Well that's a relief," Caitlin said.

"Indeed it is!" said a voice. And there was also the sound of barking and yelping.

"Bella!" Caitlin said, as Bella came round from behind the tree and stood in front of the children. "And Jack! You came to meet us."

Jack wagged his tail round and round like a helicopter rotor as the children patted him.

Bella smiled at them all. "Welcome back—again!" she said. "I thought it best to meet you here as I'd no good reason to be at your house at this precise time, Caitlin. My sources tell me it was a success. You persuaded the Prince to leave for France."

"Your sources?" Edward said.

"Yes, it was confirmed on the Eternal Vigilance website that Bonnie Prince Charlie would not be raising a new army or fighting any more battles on Scottish soil, as per the original plan. Your names are all mentioned and gratitude to you all is noted. I also had a very helpful crow, an inhabitant of a rookery on Rannoch moor apparently, who brought me notes from Lucy and from Locheil."

"And do you know if the Prince persuaded Flora Macdonald to play her part in getting him safely away to France?" Caitlin asked.

"Ah, that has still to be confirmed via the website," Bella said. "And I've no doubt it will be. But the quickest way to check out that part of the story will be for you to go home, Caitlin, and check that the locket is back in your bedside drawer."

"Yes, of course," Caitlin said. "I'll do that. And then I can text you to let you know if it is or it isn't."

"Oh, there's no need," Bella said. "I may have no excuse to be at your house just now, but I have been invited to be there this evening."

"You have?" Caitlin said.

"Yes, your father has invited me to join all of you, your brother, sister and him for a Chinese takeaway. He said that he enjoyed it so much last time we did it that he thought it would be nice to do it again." Bella beamed at Caitlin.

"Oh," Caitlin said. And she felt a bubble of happiness filling up her stomach. She smiled back at Bella.

"But right now," Bella said, "you three should get back to your homes and get some lunch."

The little group walked together to the gates of the Hermitage. Lynette and Edward led the way with Jack.

As Caitlin and Bella walked behind the others, Caitlin said. "Is your Invigilator pleased with how we did?"

"Oh, yes, I believe so," Bella replied.

"You said you'd tell me all about your boss when we got back," Caitlin said.

"Mm, I did, didn't I?" Bella frowned.

"What? " Caitlin asked.

"I don't actually know *all* about my boss. Like I said, Time Keepers don't get to meet their Invigilators. But I do have my suspicions."

"So who do you think it is?" Caitlin said.

"I'm fairly sure it's a man and I guess he's about my age and is a teacher."

"How did you guess all that?"

"His emails are short and to the point—no chit-chat¬¬—although he always mentions if he's caught a cold. He prefers to do one thing at a time, doesn't multi-task and he's more active in the school holidays. And then there's his online name."

"What is it?"

"Timetable-teacher," said Bella. "If I'm correct, it covers both his roles in life, even if it's somewhat unimaginative."

"Right." Caitlin took a minute to digest all this information. Then she had a thought. It couldn't be, could it? "Is it my history teacher, Mr Carnie?"

Bella stopped walking, as did Caitlin. "I suppose," Bella said, "yes, I suppose it could be. It would make sense. It was him who set up the history project just when you needed it." Bella began walking again. "But I really shouldn't speculate, and neither should you. Come on, we need to catch up with the others."

Once they were at the gates, Bella said, "Goodbye for now, and thank you, all three of you for all that you've done. I don't know if you will be called on again, but even if you're not, you've already done more for the good of your country and its history than most people can do in a lifetime. Well done!" And with that she walked away, waving, and with Jack trotting alongside.

"Well, that's that, then," Lynette said. "Normal life's going to be pretty dull after all this."

"Dull will be quite nice, for a while at least," Caitlin said, smiling. "And you never know, from what Bella said maybe we'll have more such adventures."

"Yes," Edward said, "but in the meantime, I better not upset my mum by being late for lunch. See you later."

Caitlin and Lynette both laughed. "See you later," they said, as Edward walked off.

When Caitlin got home, her dad called out to her as she walked in the front door. He was in his study. Caitlin went to him. He was sitting at his desk with lots of pieces of paper in front of him.

"Hello there," he said. "Have you had a nice morning with your friends?" He held his arms out to her and she went to him for a hug.

"Yes, thank you," Caitlin said.

"I was just going to stop for some lunch. I expect you're hungry too." He stood up. "Bacon roll?"

"Mmm, yes please," Caitlin said, and she followed him through to the kitchen. While he was cooking the bacon, her dad chatted to her about how she was doing at high school, about his plans for Caitlin and him at half-term, and about how it was good she was getting on so well with Bella.

Caitlin was desperate to get upstairs and check on the locket, but she was also enjoying being with her dad and getting a chance to chat like this. So she decided the checking would just have to wait until after lunch. While they ate their rolls at the kitchen table, her father told her about the Chinese meal they'd be having that evening and about inviting Bella. Caitlin acted surprised so she wouldn't have to explain about having seen Bella that morning.

"That's nice," she said. "I liked it when we had the takeaway before. Can I ask Lynette and Edward to join us?"

Dad smiled and nodded. "Yes, of course, that's an excellent idea. Fiona and James will be going out after we've eaten, and you and your friends can watch a DVD afterwards. That way Bella and I can have some time to ourselves." Dad smiled and looked as if he'd forgotten that Caitlin was there for a moment. "Yes, excellent idea," he said to himself.

"Okay," Caitlin said. "I'm going upstairs for a wee while." She got up and left her father, who still had a faraway look in his eye, sitting on his own at the table.

Caitlin picked up her rucksack from where she'd dropped it in the hall and ran upstairs to her bedroom. She pulled open the drawer in her bedside table. It was there. The little black box was there. She carefully picked it up and opened it. And there on the white silk lining was the silver locket.

With her heart thumping, she took the locket from its box and ran her fingers over the pattern on its heart-shaped surface. She clicked it open and looked at the picture of the Prince. Was he smiling more than before? She shook her head. Of course not. Then she noticed the picture seemed to have moved, come a bit loose behind its glass cover and the top was a little creased. She flicked up the glass and picked the portrait out. As she smoothed out the crease she noticed some tiny and faded writing on the back. She took it to the window so she could see it better, gasping at what was written there.

Thank you, Caitlin,
Scotland and I are forever in your debt.
Charlie.

She held it tightly. They'd succeeded. Their efforts to keep the timeline right had worked. All was as it should be.

And then she decided. She was going to wear it. That way, when Bella and the others saw her that evening, they'd know. They'd know right away that all was well. Carefully, Caitlin fastened the locket round her neck.

She unpacked her backpack and placed the library books on her desk ready to take to school on Monday. Before adding the project book to the bundle, she flicked through it. She was proud of it. They'd done a good job, her and Lynette and Edward, and not just in 1746. The project book was really good. She wondered if it had a chance of winning Mr Carnie's prize and she wondered again about Mr Carnie. She accepted what Bella said about the rules around Invigilators and their identity. And anyway, if it was Mr Carnie, that would be a good thing as she liked and respected her history teacher, and if it wasn't him, that was also okay, as whoever it was had done a good job.

She also thought how lucky she was to have two such good friends and she sent them both a text message to tell them so and to invite them both round that evening. She didn't mention the locket as she was worried one of the parents might read their messages. Lynette and Edward both replied immediately, and neither of them mentioned the locket either.

Lynette's message said, *I'm lucky to have u too. U r the best friend ever. Mum in shock coz I told her I didn't care that I look a mess J and I really dont. Theres more to life than hair straighteners. Can't wait to c u later. Got some new dance steps to show you. Lynette the Leader ;) xxx.*

Edward's reply was, *Thanks. I don't think it's luck that we're friends. I think it's that you understand me and I understand you and we like each other. I haven't had Chinese food before but I think I'd like to give it a try so I will be there. Edward.*

Caitlin smiled when she read her friends' replies. In some ways Lynette and Edward had changed since their adventure, but in other ways they were exactly the same. She supposed the same was probably true of herself too.

She sent a text message to Granny Skye to let her know that everything had worked out and said she'd call her later.

Then Caitlin lay down on her bed. She thought back over everything that had happened since she and her friends had arrived at Culloden. She thought about what it meant to be a Time Changer. She wondered what other adventures might lie ahead.

She also thought about her mum and about how she'd been a Seer. She put her hand on the locket and thought about how she missed her mum. But having the locket was very comforting. It was a link to her mother and Caitlin realised that somewhere, back along the river of time, there her mother would be, living and laughing and playing with a younger Caitlin. And Caitlin also realised that she could visit that point in the river any time in her memory.

And then, slowly and quietly at first, and then with big, loud, wrenching sobs she let herself cry for her mother. After a time the crying stopped. She felt, not good exactly, but better, sort of lighter. The big lump of sadness in her tummy felt smaller. It was all going to be okay. She was going to be okay. Before long she'd drifted off to sleep.

Sometime later she was awakened by her dad's voice bellowing up two flights of stairs, "Caitlin, can you come down please!"

She was surprised when she realised how long she'd been asleep, and after giving her hair a quick brush, she ran downstairs. The kitchen was full of people. Jack Russell gave a little yelp and ran up to her as soon as he spotted her in the doorway. As she patted him, Caitlin looked around at everyone. Her big brother and sister were sitting at the table along with Lynette and Edward. Lynette and Fiona were laughing together, looking at something on Fiona's phone, and Edward and James seemed deep in some sort of serious discussion.

But it was Dad and Bella who really caught her attention. They were standing over by the window. Bella looked amazing in a long black dress and lots of silver jewellery. And Dad—Dad appeared to wearing a new shirt and she could smell his after-shave from where she was standing. But it wasn't just his clothes that were different. It was everything—the way he was gazing at Bella as she talked—the way he was smiling and laughing—he looked sort of like the photos Caitlin had seen of him when he was a boy. It made Caitlin feel happy and sad at the same time, but she wasn't exactly sure why.

It was Lynette who first noticed Caitlin. "Hey!" she said. "At last. Come and tell Fiona what you want from the Chinese. We're all starving."

"Ah, there you are, Caiti Maiti," Dad said as he walked over to her. "You okay?" He felt her forehead and then stroked her hair. "I looked in on you earlier. You were sound asleep."

Caitlin put her arms round her dad and hugged him hard. "Yes, I'm fine. I was just a bit tired."

Dad stroked her face and smiled. "As long as you're sure. After all, you shouldn't really be tired. All you did this morning was hang around the park with your friends."

"Oh, I didn't just—that is I—"

"Come on, Caitlin, we need your order." Lynette appeared at Caitlin's side and dragged her by the arm over to where Fiona was waiting, laptop open. "Thought you needed rescuing from all that parent love," Lynette said, grinning.

Caitlin couldn't remember when she'd last felt this happy. She looked around the table at her family and friends and at Bella as they all tucked into their Chinese feast. Everyone was chatting. Fiona and Edward were discussing a scientist called Einstein. James and Lynette were talking about a band they both liked, and had been interrupted by Dad and Bella telling them the band were nowhere near as good as one they both appeared to be fans of. Caitlin realised that the big lump of sadness in her tummy had been almost completely replaced by something much lighter. She thought of her mum and although she missed her, would always miss her, it no longer hurt quite so much.

Later, when everyone had finished eating, James loaded the dishwasher without being asked. This had prompted Dad to say, "Well, this *is* a momentous day!"

"Momentous indeed," Bella said, as she winked at Caitlin and her two friends.

After James and Fiona had left for their evening out, and the others had polished off a huge tub of gorgeous caramel ice cream, Dad poured another glass of wine for himself and

Bella and said they were going through to the living-room to listen to some CDs by the band they'd been talking about. Then he put his arm round Caitlin's shoulder and said, "I got a DVD for you and Edward and Lynette to watch. It's through in the den, ready to play. And there's popcorn in the cupboard and coca-cola in the fridge for later if you want it. Oh and I checked with their parents and it's okay for your friends to sleep over, so the sleeping bags are ready in the den too." He kissed the top of her head.

Caitlin was amazed. Popcorn, coca-cola, sleepover. What had got into her dad. Whatever it was, he was different and she liked it. "Thanks, Dad," she said and she hugged him again. "Oh, by the way, what's the movie you got us?" she said as she and her friends got up to leave the kitchen.

"Ah," Dad said, grinning. "Bella chose it, but it's also an old favourite of mine. You'll love it. A bit unbelievable, but great fun. All about time travel. It's called *Back to the Future.*"

Lightning Source UK Ltd.
Milton Keynes UK
UKHW010340011221
394853UK00003B/325